Horrors We Shared The Risks of the Shared Economy

Morgan B. Blake

Published by CopyPeople.com, 2024.

Table of Contents

"The Guest in Our Home"

At first, they were thrilled about the extra income. Mark and Emily had always wanted to put their spare room to good use, and when Adam arrived, claiming to be on a business trip, they were happy to oblige. He was polite, kept to himself, and seemed harmless enough. His work as a consultant kept him busy, and he often left early in the morning and returned late in the evening. He was the perfect guest, respectful and unobtrusive—at least, that's what they thought.

But as the days passed, a strange unease began to settle into the corners of their once peaceful home. It started with the small things—the faint, almost imperceptible sound of footsteps in the hallway during the dead of night. It was never loud enough to be alarming, but just enough to disrupt the silence that usually enveloped the house after the children fell asleep.

Mark brushed it off at first. Adam was a guest, after all, and it wasn't unheard of for people to move about the house at odd hours. But then the photographs appeared.

It was Emily who found them, tucked away under Adam's bed in a small, unmarked envelope. The images were disturbing. At first, she thought she was imagining things. The children, their children—sleeping, unaware, their faces twisted into vulnerable, innocent expressions—were all there, captured in grainy, unsettling detail. The worst part wasn't just that their children had been photographed without their consent. It was the way Adam had positioned himself to take the pictures—his shadow lingering ominously on the walls, his presence so close, so intrusive, that it seemed to breathe a malignant energy into the air.

Emily's breath caught in her throat. She wanted to scream, to wake Mark, but something inside her told her to stay silent. She hid the envelope, unsure of what to do, too terrified to confront him directly.

That night, she lay awake, her mind racing. Mark slept soundly beside her, blissfully unaware of the quiet terror beginning to seep into their home. She glanced toward the guest bedroom door, which was cracked open just a sliver. The feeling of being watched crawled over her skin. She could almost hear Adam moving quietly in his room, pacing, waiting.

The next few days felt like a slow descent into madness. Emily couldn't shake the feeling that someone was watching her every move, that the walls of their house, once a sanctuary, were now closing in on her. She noticed Adam's subtle changes—the way he would linger in the kitchen too long, his gaze following her movements like a predatory animal. She felt the unease deepen, like a weight pressing down on her chest, every breath harder to take than the last.

Then the children started acting strange. Lily, the younger of the two, had begun speaking about a "man in her room," a figure who stood in the corner of her bedroom late at night, watching her sleep. At first, Emily chalked it up to a nightmare. Children often had vivid imaginations. But as Lily's drawings began to feature the shadowy figure with glowing eyes, the hairs on Emily's neck stood on end. The pieces were falling into place—too slowly, too painfully.

Emily confronted Mark about her suspicions, but he refused to believe her. He thought she was overreacting, paranoid. After all, Adam had always been friendly, even kind, and he had never given them any reason to distrust him. Mark, unable to see the terror building around them, dismissed her concerns with a kiss on the forehead and a reassuring smile. But Emily knew the truth, and every night, it became harder to ignore the suffocating dread that enveloped their home.

The breaking point came one night when Emily woke to find her daughter missing.

The house was eerily silent, the air thick with tension. She rushed to Lily's room, her heart pounding in her chest, only to find the bed empty, the covers tossed aside. Panic set in. She sprinted to the guest bedroom, her mind screaming that she had to get there, that Adam had taken Lily. But when she flung open the door, it was empty—save for a single photograph resting on the bedside table.

It was a picture of Lily, asleep in her bed, the same haunting, grainy image as before. But this time, the photograph was different. Lily's face was no longer innocent—it was twisted in terror, her eyes wide with fear. And behind her, faint but unmistakable, was Adam, his silhouette just visible in the shadows of the room.

Mark was awake now, searching frantically. But they both knew. They both understood in that moment that their worst fears had come true. Adam had taken Lily. He had been watching them, all of them, for weeks. He knew their routines, their weaknesses, their deepest vulnerabilities.

Frantically, they searched the house, but Adam was gone. There were no signs of him, no trace of where he might have taken their daughter. But in the attic, in the farthest corner of the crawl space, Emily found something—a small, locked box. Inside, there were more photographs, each one worse than the last. Pictures of their children, sleeping, crying, playing—captured at every moment of their lives, hidden away by a man they had welcomed into their home.

The house, once a place of safety, now felt like a tomb. They had opened their doors to a stranger, trusted him, shared their lives with him—and in doing so, they had unknowingly sealed their fate.

The story ended in a chilling silence. There were no answers, no resolution. The authorities would never find Adam, and the damage was irreversible. Mark and Emily were left to live in the ruins of their own naivety, their lives forever altered by the horrors of what they had shared.

In the shared economy, there are no guarantees. Trust can be a deadly thing. And for this family, there was no escape. Only the unrelenting darkness, closing in on them from every angle.

"The Tenant"

When Sarah first listed her basement apartment for rent, she never imagined that a stranger would slowly dismantle her world, piece by piece. Life had been hard enough already. As a single mother, Sarah struggled to balance work, raising two young children, and keeping the bills paid. The extra income from renting out the basement seemed like a small but necessary step toward stability. But when Thomas showed up at her door, eager, charming, and polite, she had no idea how deeply his presence would disrupt her fragile sense of peace.

Thomas was exactly what she was looking for: respectful, quiet, and hardworking. His soft-spoken demeanor and steady job gave Sarah a sense of security. He needed a place to stay for a few months while he sorted out some personal issues, he said. It was a relief to have him in the basement, especially since the children loved the idea of having a guest. At first, everything felt normal—he paid his rent on time, kept to himself, and even helped out with small tasks around the house, like fixing a leaky faucet. His presence felt harmless, even beneficial.

But then the subtle manipulations began. It started with little comments—harmless, she thought at first—that made her question her own judgment. "You've been working so hard, Sarah," he'd say with a soft smile. "Maybe you should take a break." The first time she let herself relax, allowing him to watch the kids for a few hours while she went out for a walk, she felt a fleeting sense of relief.

However, as days turned into weeks, his words began to take root in her mind. "You shouldn't be so hard on the kids," he would say. "Children need to understand discipline, but too much pressure will break them." He would offer advice that sounded helpful, yet it always felt just off—manipulative, somehow. But it was easy to ignore. She had bigger problems to deal with: mounting bills, her job that kept her away long hours, and trying to keep her children happy in a world that often seemed overwhelming.

But things began to change. Her son, Kyle, who had always been a sweet and energetic boy, began acting strangely distant. He would spend hours alone in his room, staring at the walls, his eyes unfocused. At night, he would slip out of his bed and wander the house, his bare feet barely making a sound on the floorboards. Sarah thought it was just a phase, but when she asked him what was wrong, he couldn't—wouldn't—tell her.

Her daughter, Emma, who had always been affectionate and bright, became sullen and withdrawn. She began arguing with Sarah about the smallest things, her voice sharp and cold. It was as if the warmth and love that had once existed between them had vanished overnight. Worse still, Emma started siding with Thomas during family disputes, echoing his opinions with alarming precision. Sarah had never heard her daughter speak to her in such a way—disrespectful, angry, full of accusation.

One night, Sarah overheard a conversation between Thomas and Emma as she passed by the living room. "You don't need to listen to her," Thomas was saying, his voice low, almost coaxing. "She doesn't understand. You're old enough to make your own decisions." Emma's response was barely audible, but it was enough for Sarah's heart to skip a beat. "I just want her to stop trying to control me," Emma whispered. "I wish she would let me be."

Sarah's blood ran cold. Thomas had begun to turn her children against her. He was feeding them lies, slowly eroding the bond between them, until the house felt more like a prison than a home. She confronted him about it one evening, her voice trembling with fear and anger. He was calm, too calm. "I'm only trying to help, Sarah," he said with a smile that didn't reach his eyes. "You can't keep everything in control. You need to loosen up." But his words felt like chains tightening around her chest, suffocating her.

The physical toll was beginning to show as well. Her hair started to fall out in clumps, her body growing weaker from sleepless nights filled with dread. Sarah couldn't shake the feeling that something was horribly wrong, that something unspeakable was happening in her own home. She would wake up in the middle of the night, her heart pounding, to find the house eerily silent—except for the soft sound of Thomas's footsteps in the basement, pacing back and forth, back and forth, like a predator stalking its prey.

It wasn't long before Sarah found the hidden cameras. She had always felt an odd sense of being watched, a prickling on the back of her neck whenever she entered the basement. One evening, while cleaning the laundry room, she discovered a small, hidden camera tucked behind a stack of towels. Her stomach lurched as she realized the horrifying truth: Thomas had been watching her and the children for weeks, recording their every move, studying them, manipulating them, turning them into his puppets.

Sarah tried to confront him, but by then, it was too late. Thomas had already fully embedded himself into their lives. He had ingrained himself into their routines, their hearts, their minds. He was no longer just a tenant—he was a silent, insidious force that controlled every aspect of their lives. He had already broken Sarah's children, turning them against her with his whispers, his lies, his cold touch.

One night, Sarah reached her breaking point. The house felt too small, the walls too close, the air too thick with fear. She tried to pack her things, to leave, to escape. But the moment she stepped into the basement to retrieve her bag, Thomas blocked the door, his eyes cold and unblinking. "Where do you think you're going, Sarah?" he asked, his voice calm, almost amused. "You can't leave now. You've let me in. You've already opened the door."

In that moment, Sarah realized the terrifying truth: there was no escape. The house had become a trap, and Thomas was the one holding the keys. He had already consumed everything—her trust, her family, her mind.

The story ends with Sarah standing in the basement, the walls closing in, the door locked behind her. The last thing she hears is the soft, steady hum of the camera recording, and the realization that she had given him everything—everything—and now there was no way out.

The tenant had become the master.

"The Guests in Our House"

When Clara and Jason first agreed to rent out their home to a group of "traveling professionals," they thought it would be a simple way to make some extra money. The family's kids were older now, and with the house mostly empty, it made sense to open the doors to strangers. The group was polite, professional, and seemed like the type of people anyone would trust. They had a well-dressed, corporate air about them. They came with glowing references and assured Clara and Jason that their time in the house would be short and uneventful.

At first, everything seemed fine. The guests were quiet, never causing any trouble. They came and went at odd hours, but Clara was too busy to pay much attention. It wasn't until she began noticing the changes—subtle at first—that the uneasy feeling began to creep in. The house, once full of warmth, had started to feel... different. Hollow, somehow. As if it was no longer truly theirs.

The first signs were the strange noises. At night, Clara would hear faint whispers seeping through the walls. It wasn't the sort of noise you could ignore. It felt deliberate, muffled voices speaking in an unfamiliar tongue. Jason dismissed it at first, blaming the house's creaking foundations, but the sounds grew louder, more insistent. Sometimes, in the dead of night, Clara would wake to find the living room lights flickering and the smell of incense hanging in the air, thick and sweet, like something sinister had taken root in the house.

But it was the photographs that really began to unsettle her. One morning, Clara discovered a collection of black-and-white photos strewn across the dining table. They weren't of the guests—at least, not directly—but of strange symbols, of closed doors, and images of people with hollow eyes, staring into the camera with expressions too cold, too unsettling. The images appeared to have been taken all over the house—down the hallway, in the kitchen, near the kids' bedrooms. And there was one photo in particular, placed deliberately on the top of the pile. It was of their front door—barely visible in the background, but in the foreground, something darker lingered. A figure, half-shadowed, standing on the porch, watching the house.

Jason shrugged it off, suggesting the guests had simply been playing around, but Clara couldn't shake the feeling that something was terribly wrong.

Days passed, and the family began to feel the weight of paranoia pressing down on them. The guests remained as silent as ever, but Clara and Jason found their routine disrupted. Every time they opened a door, they found things moved—slightly, unnervingly so. The couch cushions were always rearranged, the bookshelves dusted but in a way that suggested someone had been rifling through the pages. There were no footprints in the garden, no signs that anyone had been outside for fresh air. Yet, in the mornings, Clara found piles of strange objects on the kitchen counter: rocks, dried herbs, scraps of old parchment covered in cryptic symbols. Her blood ran cold as she realized these weren't just signs of normal guests; these were remnants of rituals, of practices that went far beyond mere odd behavior.

Clara confronted the guests, her voice trembling, but they only offered vague excuses. "It's a part of our work," one of them explained with a smile that didn't reach his eyes. "We require... solitude. Inspiration." They spoke of their "projects" in such cryptic terms that Clara felt herself growing dizzy with confusion. They didn't seem like professionals. They didn't seem like anything she understood. But there was no real proof of anything wrong—no tangible crime. Just the heavy, suffocating air of something evil, festering within her walls.

And then came the night the house itself seemed to scream.

Clara awoke to a loud crash in the middle of the night. Her heart hammered in her chest as she bolted from bed, rushing down the stairs to find the house plunged in darkness. The living room was an eerie sight. The guests had covered the floor with an assortment of candles—black, thick, and dripping red wax. The floor was streaked with strange markings in the light of their faint glow. At the center of the room, they stood in a circle, chanting. The voices were low, guttural, pulling at something deep inside Clara, twisting her gut into a knot.

Her children—Emma and Noah—were standing at the edge of the circle, their eyes wide and unblinking, faces pale as they watched the ritual unfold. They stood completely still, like puppets with their strings pulled too tight. Clara's breath hitched as she realized her children had been drawn into this nightmare, unaware, yet fully complicit.

"Stop!" Clara screamed, rushing toward them. But her voice was drowned out by the chanting, the words thick and alien, rising into a crescendo. Her hands trembled as she grabbed Emma, trying to pull her away, but the child's gaze was empty, vacant, as if a veil had descended over her.

It was then that Clara noticed the symbols—the ones she had seen in the photographs—scrawled in fresh blood on the walls, beneath the cold light of the flickering candles. The house had become something else, a dark altar, a stage for an unimaginable horror. Her mind reeled, trying to grasp what was happening, but the room seemed to close in on her, suffocating her.

Jason rushed in, but by then, it was too late. He was swept into the circle by the guests, who seemed to have changed, their once calm, professional demeanor now twisted into something monstrous. Clara could hear the strange clicking noises they made with their throats, their smiles too wide, too sharp. They had become something else entirely—predators, possessors, like parasites feeding off her fear.

She stumbled back, the weight of their collective gaze closing in. Her body screamed to run, but the house felt like a cage, the walls shifting, closing in tighter and tighter. There was nowhere left to go. The rituals, the photographs, the strange symbols—all of it had been building to this moment. The final offering, the final possession. Clara and her family had opened the door to this madness by trusting strangers in their home.

As Clara was pulled back into the dark embrace of the circle, her final thought was a chilling one: The house would never be the same. And neither would she.

"A Taste of Poison"

Lena and David had spent years building their small but successful catering business, "True Flavor," from the ground up. What had started as a shared dream had evolved into a well-established brand in their local community. The kitchen they rented had always been their sanctuary, the place where they poured their hearts into their dishes. But as business expanded, so did the need for more space—more equipment, more resources, and most urgently, more time.

When Adam, a fellow chef they met through a local food network, offered to rent their kitchen space during off-hours, it seemed like a golden opportunity. He was polite, experienced, and claimed to be working on his own culinary creations. They were happy to help out a fellow chef, and the extra income would allow them to invest in new equipment.

At first, everything seemed to go smoothly. Adam was quiet but efficient, often leaving the kitchen spotless after each shift. He brought in his own ingredients—exotic spices and powders, jars of oils they'd never seen before—and kept to himself for the most part. But there was something off about him, something Lena couldn't quite place. The way his eyes flickered with a strange intensity when he spoke about food, the way he'd insist on handling certain ingredients or methods that seemed odd to her, though she never questioned him too much. He was a professional, after all.

But soon, things began to change. It started subtly at first—small things Lena couldn't put her finger on. The air in the kitchen began to smell... wrong. It wasn't the comforting, inviting aroma of simmering stocks or fresh herbs. It was sharper, acrid, a strange metallic scent that lingered long after Adam had left. Lena mentioned it to David once, but he just shrugged it off. "It's probably just the new spices he's using," he said. "Chef's always got something weird in the works."

The first real warning came a week later when Lena began to feel nauseous after a long day in the kitchen. Her stomach twisted painfully, and her head swam with dizziness. At first, she thought it was just the stress of their growing business and the extra work they had been putting in. But when David started complaining of the same symptoms—headaches, fever, and an unshakable sense of weakness—Lena grew concerned. They both shrugged it off, assuming they were just coming down with a cold or exhaustion. But things only worsened.

One evening, Lena went into the kitchen to prep for the next day's orders. She was already feeling light-headed, but what she saw in the kitchen took her breath away. Adam had left behind his equipment—cooking tools that were covered in strange, sticky residues. There were powdery white substances spilled on the counter, scattered around containers of thick, foul-smelling liquids. It wasn't food—it was something else. Something chemical. Lena's heart pounded as her eyes scanned the mess.

A small vial, clear but reflecting an unnatural light, sat open on the counter. The label had been smudged, but it was still visible—"Methamphetamine, pure." Lena recoiled, her hand flying to her mouth as nausea overtook her. Her eyes widened in horror as she realized what was happening. Adam wasn't just cooking meals; he was using the kitchen to produce illegal substances. The very place they had built their business, their dreams, was now tainted.

The walls of the kitchen seemed to close in on her, the air thick with something toxic, suffocating. It wasn't just a betrayal—it was an invasion, a violation of the safe space they had worked so hard to create. Lena felt as though she were choking on the smell, her body rebelling against the reality of what she had discovered. She backed away from the counter, her mind racing. She needed to tell David. She needed to do something, anything to stop it before it destroyed everything.

But as she reached the door, her vision blurred, and her knees buckled beneath her. She collapsed on the cold floor, the room spinning wildly around her. She could hear her pulse thundering in her ears, her breath shallow and ragged. It felt like something was crawling beneath her skin, a fire spreading through her veins, hot and painful.

David found her moments later, his face pale, his eyes filled with the same terror. He, too, collapsed beside her, his body wracked with uncontrollable shivers. The world around them seemed to distort, a nightmare unfolding in slow motion as they both struggled to breathe. It wasn't just exhaustion or a flu. They were poisoned.

They made it to the hospital, where they were both treated for severe chemical exposure. The doctors couldn't determine the exact cause of their symptoms, but they warned them that it could have been deadly had they waited any longer. Adam was gone by the time they returned to the kitchen. His belongings were packed, and the place was eerily silent, empty.

The next few days were a blur. Lena and David couldn't shake the feeling that something was horribly wrong, that they had been dragged into a nightmare from which there was no escape. As they recovered, they received a call from the authorities. The police had seized their kitchen equipment, claiming it had been used for illegal drug production. The equipment, once a symbol of their hard work, was now evidence in a criminal investigation.

Their business, built over years of sweat and sacrifice, was destroyed. Their reputation was tarnished. The damage was irreversible. Orders were canceled, clients abandoned them, and soon, their accounts were frozen under suspicion of involvement in the illegal operation. All they had worked for—gone in the blink of an eye.

It wasn't just the financial ruin that haunted them. It was the lingering fear that they had opened their doors to a predator, and in doing so, had allowed their lives to be destroyed. The kitchen, once a place of creation, was now a dark memory, a symbol of betrayal. The worst part was knowing they would never truly escape the shadow Adam had cast over them. Their business was gone. Their future, uncertain.

And as the authorities continued their investigation, Lena and David were left alone, trapped in a web of suspicion, guilt, and regret, haunted by the realization that the shared economy, which they had so blindly trusted, had been their downfall.

"Through the Walls"

When Anna first met Eric, she thought he was a godsend. Her apartment had always felt too big for one person, and the rising costs of living in the city had made it difficult to make ends meet. Eric was polite, respectful, and seemed like an ordinary man in his early thirties. He told her he had just moved to town for work, a tech job that kept him on the road most of the time. He needed a quiet, affordable place to stay while he adjusted to life in the city. Anna liked that he was quiet, that he kept to himself. She needed peace—especially after a painful divorce that left her feeling vulnerable, uncertain.

The first few weeks were uneventful. Eric moved in, paid his rent on time, and kept to his room. Anna noticed that he spent a lot of time in front of his laptop, but she didn't think much of it. It was the digital age, after all—everyone was glued to their screens. It wasn't until she began feeling a strange unease around the house that she started to take notice.

It started with the doors. One evening, Anna walked into the kitchen to find the door to her bedroom slightly ajar. She swore she had closed it earlier, but she brushed it off, chalking it up to her own forgetfulness. A few days later, it happened again. Her door wasn't just ajar; it was wide open, as if someone had been inside while she was out. The door had a lock, but something about the state of it made her uneasy. A creeping suspicion started to grow in the back of her mind, but she couldn't put her finger on it.

Then there were the cameras.

It was late one evening when Anna returned home from work and noticed a small, nearly invisible black dot nestled in the corner of the living room ceiling. She'd always been meticulous about the space—she knew every inch of her apartment, and this camera, no matter how well-hidden, was out of place. Panic surged through her. She ran to her bedroom, yanking open the drawer to find her phone and check the security settings. But there was nothing. No alert. No warning. The camera was still there, unobtrusive, blending with the dark corners of the room.

The fear twisted in her stomach. She didn't confront Eric immediately. What could she say? She had no proof, no concrete evidence that he was doing anything wrong. But over the next few days, her paranoia heightened. Every time she walked into a room, her gaze would flicker to the corners, to the ceilings, searching for those little black dots. Her eyes no longer felt safe; her own home felt like a prison, an extension of someone else's voyeuristic desire.

It wasn't until Anna stumbled upon something she wasn't supposed to see that the full horror became clear.

She had come home early from work, a rare occasion, and found Eric in the living room, his laptop open in front of him. He hadn't heard her approach. His focus was intense, his eyes fixed on the screen. But when she stepped into the doorway, her breath caught in her throat. On the screen was footage—of her. Of *her*—sitting on the couch, eating dinner, reading a book, moving around the apartment. But the most unsettling part was how the footage was arranged. It wasn't just one shot, one angle. It was as if every corner of her home had been captured. Every movement. Every private moment. He had orchestrated this from the shadows.

Her heart raced as Eric quickly closed the laptop, his eyes flashing with a brief flicker of guilt, before he masked it with a smile. "I was just setting up the system," he said, his voice smooth, too smooth. "You know, for security. To make sure nothing happens when I'm away. The neighborhood can be dangerous."

His explanation was too perfect, too rehearsed. The words hit Anna like a slap, but she couldn't respond. She was paralyzed with shock. The walls seemed to close in, pressing in on her chest as the reality of what had been happening finally sank in. The cameras, the strange doors, the feeling of being watched—it had all been part of his plan. And now, her privacy, her very being, had been commodified by someone who had invaded her space, her life, without her consent.

Over the following weeks, Anna tried to avoid him. She kept her head down, pretending to be busy, pretending everything was fine. But every night, when the house fell silent, the dread crept back. The camera angles. The unsettling footage. Her every movement dissected. It felt like she was no longer in control of her own life, no longer in control of her own body.

But the true nightmare hadn't yet begun.

One evening, Anna's worst fear was realized when she logged into her email to find a message from an anonymous account. The subject line was simple: *"Your life, for sale."* She opened it, her hand trembling. The message contained a link, and when she clicked on it, her heart stopped.

There, on the screen, was a website. Her website. Her private moments—the footage from the cameras—had been uploaded. The most intimate, the most personal. Her face, her body, her actions—exploited for profit. She couldn't breathe. Her mind couldn't comprehend the horror. Someone was watching. Someone was paying for access to her life, her dignity. And the worst part was, it wasn't just her. Eric had sold the footage to dozens of people, as if she were nothing more than a spectacle for their pleasure.

Lena tried to report it to the authorities, but the damage had already been done. The videos were already viral, already circulating across the dark web. There was no stopping it. There was no escaping it. Her life, once so simple, had been irrevocably altered by a man she had trusted. A man she had welcomed into her home, into her life.

The walls closed in on her, and she realized with sickening clarity that she could never feel safe again. The shared economy, which promised connection and trust, had stripped her of everything. Her body, her privacy, her identity—everything had been sold to the highest bidder, and there was no undoing it. The worst part wasn't even the exposure. It was the realization that she had been living in a house of glass, and someone had been watching her the entire time. Every move, every breath, captured in the silence.

She would never escape the eyes of the world. She was a prisoner in her own skin.

"The Guests We Invited"

The Baxter family had always been a close-knit group, a loving family of four living in a quiet suburban neighborhood. They had a modest home, filled with memories and laughter, but with rising expenses, it had become increasingly difficult to keep up. The idea of renting out their living room space for extra income seemed harmless enough—a way to help cover bills without disrupting their daily lives too much. The space was cozy, located at the back of the house, with a private entrance and its own bathroom. They advertised it online, offering it as a temporary solution for people who needed a place to stay while they were passing through the area.

At first, the guests who came and went seemed perfectly normal. There was Jane, a middle-aged woman who needed a room for a few weeks while she worked on a local project. Then there was Brian, a quiet man who seemed a little reserved but polite. The Baxters were happy with the arrangement; they were earning extra income, and the guests respected their home. They began to let their guard down, comforted by the belief that these strangers would stay for only short periods of time.

But then came him—Victor.

He was the one who seemed to linger too long, the one who began to make their home feel like it wasn't truly theirs anymore. He was polite at first, his mannerisms a bit too perfect, too practiced. He seemed to respect their boundaries—never crossing any lines, always appearing to keep to himself. His presence, however, began to unsettle them in ways they couldn't fully explain. He'd often linger too long at the kitchen table, always watching the family, always too silent. His eyes would follow them in ways that were far too intense, as if he could see through their skin, through their thoughts. He never seemed to have much to say, and yet, there was an air about him that made every interaction feel strained, as if something was hanging just beneath the surface, waiting to explode.

It wasn't long before strange things started happening. Small things, at first. Items would go missing or be moved around, like the family's personal belongings had been touched. At night, they would hear faint scraping sounds coming from the living room—almost like the scratching of metal against the floor. It didn't make sense. Victor wasn't supposed to be there; he had a job in town during the day. Yet, the sounds persisted, always at odd hours when the family was asleep.

The first time the Baxters found a bloodstain on the carpet, it was barely noticeable—just a small, dark splotch in the corner, beneath a chair. It could have been anything, they thought. It could have been an accident, a spill that hadn't been cleaned properly. But the stain grew over the following weeks. It spread, as if it had soaked into the fibers of the carpet, never fully gone. And the smell, faint but distinct, began to linger. The family assumed it was just old carpet, nothing more. But deep down, they felt an instinctive, gnawing discomfort.

Clara, the mother, tried to talk to Victor about the strange occurrences. He reassured her with an almost eerie calmness, apologizing for the inconvenience and promising it would never happen again. He was quick to dismiss her concerns, his eyes too still, too controlled. But when she mentioned the bloodstain, his expression shifted—just for a moment. It was subtle, but Clara caught it. A flicker of something sinister crossed his face, as though she had said something she wasn't supposed to know.

Then came the night when everything unraveled.

Clara woke to the sound of muffled voices in the living room, though it was past midnight. She quietly crept down the hallway, thinking perhaps Victor was having a late-night conversation with someone on the phone. But when she reached the living room, what she saw froze her in place.

Victor was standing in the middle of the room, but he wasn't alone. Another man—stranger, disheveled—was sitting on the couch, bound and gagged. The man's eyes were wide with fear, his body trembling, soaked in sweat. Clara's breath caught in her throat as she watched Victor, calm and collected, as he moved toward the man. His voice was barely audible, but it was clear that he was speaking to him with authority, as if he had done this before. His hands, now stained with something dark, worked methodically, almost clinically, as he prepared the man for something that was impossible to comprehend.

Clara's mind raced, but her body felt paralyzed. She wanted to scream, to run, but all she could do was stand there, trembling. In that moment, the reality of what was happening hit her like a hammer. Victor wasn't just a guest. He wasn't just a man looking for a place to stay. He was something far darker. The house, their home, had become a place of horror, a place where unspeakable things were taking place beneath the surface of their everyday lives.

She turned to leave, to warn her family, but she had made a mistake. As she reached the hallway, she felt a cold hand wrap around her wrist, pulling her back into the living room. Victor's face was twisted with a quiet, unsettling grin.

"I think you've seen enough," he whispered, his voice smooth and deadly. "But there's still so much more I need to show you."

The next few hours were a blur. Clara's mind struggled to process what was happening, but she couldn't escape. Every time she thought she had a chance, the walls seemed to close in tighter. The house was no longer hers; it had become a nightmare, and she was trapped in it. Victor's work continued, his every action calculated, precise. He had lured people into their home, unsuspecting, desperate, using the place to conceal his true nature. The smell of death was in the air, a lingering presence that filled every room, every corner.

And then, just as quickly as he had come, Victor was gone. The family was left in the aftermath of his horrors—his victims, his crimes, his twisted game. The police arrived, but by then, it was too late. The damage had been done. The Baxters were left with nothing but broken minds, shattered lives, and a house forever stained by the darkest of secrets.

Victor had disappeared without a trace, leaving nothing behind but the ghostly memories of what they had allowed into their home. And the worst part? They would never be free of the consequences of the shared economy. No matter how far they ran, no matter how much they tried to forget, the stain of what had happened there would remain with them forever.

"The Price of Kindness"

Sophie and Daniel had always believed in the goodness of their community. The small, quiet neighborhood where they had bought their house years ago was tight-knit. The neighbors were friendly, always looking out for one another, and the air was thick with the scent of home-cooked meals and freshly mowed lawns. As a young couple with dreams of starting a family, Sophie and Daniel were grateful for the support of their neighbors. So, when they decided to open their kitchen to share their food with others, it felt like the right thing to do. They had a spacious kitchen, a garden brimming with vegetables, and enough love for all.

The couple invited a few neighbors over for dinner one evening, offering food made with ingredients from their own backyard. The guests, a few families from down the block, were grateful for the gesture. The evening was full of laughter, shared stories, and the warmth that comes from breaking bread together. Sophie and Daniel were happy. Their home felt alive with connection and trust, and they knew they had made the right choice.

But after that night, something began to shift. It was subtle at first—small things they hadn't noticed before. Sophie found an extra set of dirty dishes in the sink the next morning, even though no one had been there since the night before. Daniel, too, began noticing things out of place: spices moved from one shelf to another, ingredients from the pantry mysteriously disappearing. He blamed it on his own forgetfulness, or maybe the kids had been playing in the kitchen. But deep down, there was an uncomfortable feeling gnawing at both of them, a strange sensation that the house was no longer entirely their own.

It wasn't until the smell began to change that they realized how far things had gone.

One evening, Sophie returned home from the grocery store to a thick, pungent odor that hit her the moment she walked in the door. It wasn't the familiar, comforting scent of fresh herbs or roasting vegetables. It was something sharper, chemical—an acrid, almost sickening scent that made her stomach churn. She immediately went into the kitchen to investigate, but there was no one there. The smell was overpowering, clinging to the air like a thick fog. Sophie's breath caught in her throat as she looked around, trying to identify the source.

On the countertop, she noticed something out of place—a strange powdery residue, fine and white, scattered near the sink. She bent closer, feeling a twinge of nausea rise in her throat. The powder had an unnatural, almost fluorescent glow in the dim light. Her heart pounded in her chest as she scanned the rest of the kitchen. The cabinets were half-open, the floor littered with strange substances she didn't recognize. Bottles of liquid chemicals—some of them half-empty—lined the counter. Some were labeled, but the names were foreign, written in a language she couldn't read. The terrifying realization hit her like a wave: this wasn't just food prep. This was something far darker.

Panicking, she called Daniel, but when he arrived, his face went pale the moment he stepped into the kitchen. His eyes darted around, taking in the scene, and for a moment, they both stood frozen, as if unable to process the nightmare unfolding around them. There were traces of chemicals everywhere—on the countertops, on the cutting board, in the sink. It was as though the very essence of their home, their sanctuary, had been taken over by something vile. The food they had lovingly prepared for their neighbors, the warmth of their home, had been turned into a twisted space where something sinister was being created.

Daniel quickly went to the pantry, hoping against hope that the damage was contained. But as soon as he opened the door, his hand recoiled in disgust. The shelves were lined with bags of substances—brown powder, crystalline particles, and bags of what looked like dried plants. The labels on some of them were smudged, others were completely blank, but the ominous feeling in the pit of Daniel's stomach told him everything he needed to know. Their kitchen was being used as a drug lab.

Sophie, her hands shaking, stumbled back into the living room. The weight of the discovery settled over her like a suffocating fog. The people they had invited into their home, the neighbors they had trusted, had been using their kitchen to prepare illicit drugs. And worse yet, their home, the place they had opened up to others, had become a sanctuary for criminal activity. They had no idea how far it went. How long it had been going on.

In the days that followed, the couple began noticing more signs of intrusion. Sophie's careful attempts to clean the kitchen seemed futile. Every time she scrubbed the countertops, the chemical smell returned stronger than before. They found small, barely noticeable stains on the walls, yellowish smears that had no logical explanation. Every time Daniel tried to cook, the stench lingered, poisoning the food they tried to prepare. Their sanctuary had become a nightmare, a place where they were no longer welcome.

The psychological toll was just as severe. Sophie's paranoia grew, her mind spiraling into fear. They began to feel watched, as if someone was always in the house, observing their every move. Their neighbors, once so friendly, became distant, their interactions strange and curt. Sophie couldn't shake the feeling that they knew—knew what had been happening in her home—and were now turning away from her in silent judgment. The tension between her and Daniel grew unbearable. How could they have been so blind? How could they have invited this evil into their home?

But the worst part was when they realized there was no escape. The authorities arrived, their suspicions raised by an anonymous tip. They swept through the house, seizing everything—every pot, every utensil, every ingredient. The Baxters were told their home was now a crime scene, tainted by the presence of dangerous chemicals. The family's livelihood was destroyed. Their reputation, their entire life, was shattered in an instant.

They moved out, their lives in ruins, but the damage was irreversible. They couldn't escape the lingering effects—the physical and emotional scars left behind by the chemicals. The damage to their health was insidious, their bodies slowly deteriorating from prolonged exposure to the substances that had been prepared in their kitchen. Sophie couldn't shake the feeling that they were being watched, still, by eyes they could never escape. And as they left their house for good, they realized the terrifying truth:

There was no safety, no sanctity, in sharing your space. The shared economy had turned their home into a nightmare, one they could never truly wake from.

"The House That Was Never Ours"

The cabin was meant to be a dream—an escape from the pressures of everyday life, a place where a group of friends could gather, reconnect, and celebrate their shared history. Tucked away in the woods, surrounded by tall pine trees, the secluded vacation home had been in the group for years. It was an escape, a place to relax, laugh, and make memories. But when money became tight, they decided to rent it out for the weekend to cover expenses. They never imagined the decision would lead them into a nightmare.

The group—Sarah, Mark, Lydia, and Sam—had always trusted one another. They were close-knit, their friendships forged over years of college and late-night conversations. They'd been planning this weekend for months. It was supposed to be the perfect getaway: a break from work, a chance to unwind, and an opportunity to rekindle the bonds that had begun to fray with time.

When the rental request came through, it seemed harmless enough. A couple, Claire and Daniel, needed a weekend escape. They seemed polite in their messages, respectful of the house rules. They even offered to pay a little extra for cleaning services. The group agreed, pleased that they could make a little extra money.

The first night, things seemed normal. Claire and Daniel arrived late, only briefly exchanging pleasantries before heading into the house. The friends stayed on the porch, enjoying the crisp air, laughing as the fire pit crackled. But as the night stretched on, something felt... off. The house was quieter than usual. The energy, once alive with their chatter, now seemed stifled, almost suffocating.

The next morning, Sarah went inside to prepare breakfast and noticed something strange in the kitchen. The counter was covered in plastic sheeting, a stark contrast to the rustic charm the house usually had. The faint smell of bleach lingered in the air. At first, she chalked it up to the guests being overly cautious—perhaps cleaning up from something. But as she started to clean the countertops, her eyes fell on a discarded rubber glove, stained with something dark.

"Mark," she called, her voice tight with unease.

Mark walked in, glancing at the plastic sheeting. He frowned but said nothing. They decided to shake it off, assuming it was just an odd habit of their guests.

By the second night, however, the unease had deepened.

The evening began with the usual fun. Drinks flowed, stories were shared, and the friends tried to ignore the growing discomfort. But as the hours passed, they began noticing things. Claire and Daniel were nowhere to be seen. Their bedroom door was always shut, and the faint sound of muffled conversations came from behind it—voices low, too muffled to make out. When Sam went to knock, the door swung open to reveal nothing more than a pristine room, the bed neatly made as if untouched.

That's when things started to unravel.

The friends had always known the house had its quirks. Old pipes that groaned, creaky floors that had a way of telling you when someone was moving around. But now, the sounds in the house were different. The whispers, the shifting, the low hum of something electrical—it wasn't normal. It felt like they were being watched, their every move scrutinized by invisible eyes.

The next morning, Lydia went to the basement to retrieve some extra blankets and stumbled upon something that made her stomach churn. Tucked behind the washing machine was a stack of strange, black duffel bags. They were out of place, too heavy for their size. Her hand trembled as she unzipped one, only to pull back in shock when she saw what was inside: bags of chemicals. Not just any chemicals—dangerous substances, some of them labeled with warnings she couldn't read. And there were more bags behind them. Boxes filled with things she couldn't name but knew were wrong.

Her breath caught in her throat as she stumbled backward, her mind racing. This wasn't a vacation. This wasn't a couple on a weekend getaway. They had been drawn into something far darker.

Panic spread through the group like wildfire. Mark immediately called the police, but as soon as the sirens were heard in the distance, Claire and Daniel were gone—vanished into the woods, leaving no trace behind. The bags remained, sitting there in the basement like a horrifying reminder of their mistake.

The police arrived and began their investigation, but the damage had already been done. It wasn't just the illegal substances they had to deal with—it was the aftermath of what had been done in the house. The walls were lined with hidden cameras, some disguised as everyday objects—lights, picture frames, even smoke detectors. Claire and Daniel had turned the house into their operation base, using it not only to store drugs but to track their victims—recording everything.

The friends couldn't escape the feeling of violation, of being trapped in a house that was no longer their own. The atmosphere was thick with dread, as though the walls themselves had absorbed the horrors of what had taken place there. They were left to face the consequences of their ignorance—of their willingness to trust strangers. The police uncovered everything: the operation, the drugs, the surveillance footage—but there was something else, too. The bodies. Hidden, discarded, left behind by those who had once been guests in their home. The house, once a sanctuary, had become a graveyard.

The friends tried to return to normalcy, but it was impossible. They couldn't unsee the evidence, couldn't erase the haunting memories of the cameras, the chemicals, the bloodstains they couldn't scrub out. They were trapped—not just by the house but by the knowledge that they had been complicit, even if unknowingly. Every creak of the floorboards, every flicker of light reminded them of the terror they had welcomed into their lives.

It was too late to run. The shared economy had destroyed them. The line between safety and danger had been blurred, and they had allowed it to happen. They couldn't escape the knowledge that their lives would never be the same, that the shadows of the past would follow them forever.

And so, they left the house—though the house had already left them. No matter where they went, no matter how far they ran, the fear would remain. The shared economy had promised connection and opportunity, but instead, it had given them a nightmare from which there was no waking.

"The Ride You Never Asked For"

Emily had always been an easy-going person. She was trusting, open, and always willing to lend a hand when someone needed it. So when Daniel, a man who had just moved into her neighborhood, asked if he could borrow her car for a few hours, she didn't hesitate. She had heard that car-sharing was becoming more common, especially in their community, and she was more than happy to help. After all, he seemed like a harmless man—polite, clean-cut, and courteous.

He explained he was having car trouble and just needed to run a quick errand. "I'll return it in a few hours, I promise," he said, his voice reassuring, his smile warm. Emily handed him the keys without thinking twice.

The car was a small sedan, nothing fancy, but it was her lifeline—she depended on it for work, for grocery runs, for everything. It wasn't just a mode of transport; it was a piece of her world, and trusting Daniel with it was an act of kindness she rarely hesitated to extend.

But hours passed, and there was no word from him. Emily tried calling, but the calls went unanswered. By the time the sun began to set, a gnawing unease settled in her chest. She told herself she was being paranoid—he'd probably gotten stuck in traffic, or maybe he was running late. Still, the weight of her growing suspicion made her feel like something was off.

Then came the knock on the door. The police.

At first, Emily didn't understand. They had found her car. Her car, which she had let Daniel borrow. It was parked on the side of the road, near the outskirts of town, surrounded by crime scene tape. Emily felt her heart stop, her blood run cold. She stepped outside, her feet unsteady, her body moving of its own accord, drawn to the horror that awaited her. She was confronted by a detective who asked her questions that made her head spin. Was she familiar with Daniel? Where had he gone? When had she last seen him?

"Daniel?" she stammered, her throat tight. "I just... I let him borrow my car. I didn't know..."

The detective's face darkened as he looked at her with a mix of pity and suspicion. "Your car has been used in a series of kidnappings. Three people are missing. We need to ask you more questions."

The words hit her like a freight train, but it wasn't until she saw the footage that everything clicked into place. The police had surveillance footage from several cameras on the route Daniel had taken. The car was spotted near an isolated area, parked alongside the road. In the footage, Daniel could be seen pulling out of the car and walking toward a woman who was standing at a bus stop. Within seconds, the woman was dragged into the car. The sight was chilling. The footage, grainy but unmistakable, showed Daniel's cold, calculated actions, his hand clamped over the woman's mouth as he shoved her into the car.

But it wasn't just one victim. In the following hours, the car was used again. Another woman. Another kidnapping. And yet another. The camera's angle was just enough to catch glimpses of the terror in their eyes as they were driven away, helpless and panicked.

Emily was in shock. This was her car. Her car had become an instrument of terror. The place where she had spent countless hours driving to work, picking up groceries, driving to family gatherings—now it was a crime scene, a vessel of suffering. And she had unknowingly handed it over to someone who would use it to destroy lives.

As the days passed, the weight of what had happened settled on her like a dark cloud. The police had confiscated her car, leaving her stranded. She couldn't go anywhere, couldn't live her life without constant reminders of the nightmare that had unfolded. Every time she turned on the news, there were reports of missing people, their faces plastered across the screen, their families devastated. All of them had been in her car. Her *car*. The thought that she had been unknowingly complicit in their abductions gnawed at her, churning in her stomach like a poison she couldn't expel.

The worst part wasn't just the guilt, though. It was the realization that Daniel had been so close, so *normal*. She had trusted him with the most important thing in her life, her own means of transportation, and now she could never trust anyone again. That small act of kindness had shattered her sense of safety. She had opened the door to evil without even realizing it.

It wasn't just the horror of what Daniel had done with her car. It was the aftermath—the slow, suffocating realization that the world she knew had been turned upside down. Every time she looked at her hands, she saw them stained with the unintentional blood of the innocent. Every time she went outside, she could feel eyes on her, as if the entire world now saw her as complicit in the crime. She couldn't go anywhere without hearing whispers behind her back, without feeling like people were judging her, wondering how she could be so *blind* to the danger she had invited into her life.

Daniel was eventually caught, but by then it didn't matter. He had already taken everything from her—her trust, her peace of mind, her safety. He had used her kindness against her, turning her once simple, innocent gesture into a horrific nightmare she could never escape. The memories of those terrified faces, those helpless victims, haunted her. And the worst part was, the echoes of the kidnapping spree would never stop. Her car, her *safe space*, would always be a reminder of the twisted fate she had unwittingly brought upon herself and others.

In the end, there was no resolution. No happy closure. There were no neat, tidy conclusions. Emily was left to live in a world where her actions, her kindness, had unintentionally led to suffering. There was no forgiveness for herself, no way to erase the images, the sounds, the terror. The consequences of sharing her car had forever altered the course of her life, and there was no way to outrun the shadow that now loomed over her.

And as the sun set, casting long, dark shadows across the empty streets, Emily couldn't shake the feeling that somewhere, out there, someone else was waiting. Waiting for the next victim to trust them, to offer them something for free, to open their doors and their hearts just one more time. And when they did, the darkness would swallow them whole.

"The Tenants"

Max had always been a bit of a loner. He spent his days working from home as a freelance graphic designer, his nights lost in books and quiet music. The apartment was small, tucked into the heart of a quiet, middle-class neighborhood where everything seemed calm and untouched by the chaos of the outside world. He kept to himself, rarely speaking to the neighbors, and life was simple.

That was until the couple arrived.

They came looking for a temporary place to stay, just a few months while they transitioned to a new city. They were well-dressed, articulate, and seemed to have an air of sophistication about them—Sarah and Marcus. They spoke with confidence, their eyes steady and calm, their smiles warm but distant. Max, always eager to make a little extra cash, agreed to rent the apartment to them. They assured him they wouldn't be any trouble. The rent was good, and they seemed harmless enough. Besides, they were polite and gave no indication of being anything other than a young couple just looking for a place to live.

The first few weeks passed without incident. Max noticed nothing out of the ordinary, but a creeping feeling of unease began to settle over him. There were oddities—small things at first—that began to unsettle him. The strange symbols on the welcome mat outside his door, like they had been scrawled hurriedly in chalk and then washed away by rain, went unnoticed by most. At night, he would hear faint murmurs from within the apartment—voices that seemed to grow louder as if Sarah and Marcus were discussing something just beyond his reach. He couldn't make out the words, but the sound of their low tones filled the hallways, reverberating like a drumbeat in the otherwise silent building.

One evening, Max's curiosity got the better of him. He decided to stop by unannounced to see how they were settling in. His heart raced as he approached the apartment door, an inexplicable sense of dread beginning to claw at him. When he knocked, Marcus answered immediately, his face beaming with an unnervingly serene smile.

"Oh, Max! How nice to see you," Marcus said, his voice too smooth, too welcoming. "We were just about to have a little gathering. Would you like to join us?"

Max hesitated, but the invitation felt too polite to decline. "Sure," he said, trying to keep his voice steady. "Why not?"

The moment he stepped inside, something hit him—a pungent, overpowering odor that made his stomach twist. It wasn't unpleasant, but it was thick and earthy, a strange scent of incense and something he couldn't quite place. The apartment felt... different. Darker somehow. The air was heavy, thick with an unspoken tension. The room itself was decorated in ways that unsettled him. There were tapestries on the walls with strange, almost hypnotic patterns, and candles—too many candles—burning in every corner of the room. The flickering shadows danced around, distorting the space into something otherworldly.

The couple welcomed him warmly, but their eyes held a strange intensity, an unsettling focus that felt almost invasive. They offered him tea, which he politely accepted, though he couldn't help but notice the strange liquid swirling in the cup. It was dark, almost black, and the steam rising from it smelled sweet, cloying. The moment he took a sip, his throat tightened, and his head spun.

He tried to ignore the feeling, but it only worsened. The room began to spin. The walls seemed to close in around him, the flickering candles growing more intense, casting long, distorting shadows on the walls. He turned to Sarah, but her face had changed. Her eyes, once calm, were now wide with a fervor he couldn't place.

And then they spoke.

"The ritual is nearly complete," Sarah said, her voice low and reverberating with something he couldn't understand. "We need a sacrifice, Max. You've given us so much. We're so grateful for the space you've provided, the vessel you've offered."

Max's heart raced. His breath came in shallow gasps as the dizziness overtook him. What were they talking about? What ritual? He tried to get up, but his body refused to obey. His muscles felt like stone. He tried to speak, but the words caught in his throat.

As the haze in his mind cleared, he realized the truth—it wasn't just incense in the air. The apartment had been transformed into something unrecognizable. Strange symbols had been painted on the walls, etched into the floor in thick, dark strokes. The ceiling was covered in a large, circular drawing, with intricate markings around it. The space was a shrine, a place where something terrible was about to take place.

They weren't just tenants. They weren't just a couple. They were *something else.*

Max's panic was palpable. His pulse thundered in his ears as he tried to stand, to escape, but his legs buckled beneath him. His hands were shaking, and his vision blurred. Marcus stepped forward, a calm smile spreading across his face, his hands moving in slow, deliberate gestures, as if performing some ritual Max had no hope of understanding.

"We've been waiting for this moment," Marcus said, his eyes gleaming with an unnerving intensity. "You've allowed us the space we need. You've given us everything."

And then, as if orchestrated by some unseen hand, the doors to the apartment slammed shut. The windows, once clear, began to fog over, the room suffocating under the weight of unseen forces. The couple moved toward him, their movements synchronized, too perfect, too controlled.

Max tried to scream, but the air was thick with pressure. His mouth was dry, his vision fading. The walls seemed to pulse, the floor beneath him trembling as though something was awakening from beneath the building.

And then, as the room went dark, he heard them speak again.

"We only need your blood, Max. You're our final offering."

The ritual had begun.

The next morning, when the building manager arrived to check on the apartment, there was nothing left of Max. The door to his unit was locked, but the faintest sound of chanting could still be heard from the inside. His apartment, once a safe, quiet space, had become a house of horrors—its walls now soaked in dark stains, the strange symbols still glowing faintly in the dim light of the morning.

Max was gone, lost to the madness his own kindness had unwittingly allowed.

The couple, Sarah and Marcus, had left the apartment in the dead of night, taking all traces of their existence with them. The police found nothing, no record of the couple, no trace of their true names. They had disappeared into the ether, their ritual complete, leaving Max's apartment as a hollow shell—haunted by the terrifying realization that the shared economy had given way to something far darker.

For the next tenants, it would be the same. The apartment was no longer a simple place to live. It was a vessel, a gateway for something far worse. And no one would ever truly escape the consequences of opening the door to the wrong strangers.

"The Guest in the Room"

Lauren and Mark had always been kind-hearted people, willing to extend a hand to anyone in need. Their house was modest but comfortable, nestled on a quiet street in a sleepy neighborhood. When they first put the spare bedroom up for rent, it seemed like a good idea—a way to help out, make some extra cash, and meet new people. They never imagined how the decision would slowly unravel their lives.

Anna came to them with a calm demeanor and an air of politeness that put them at ease. She was in her mid-thirties, well-spoken, and appeared normal, even charming. She explained that she had recently moved to the area for work and needed a temporary place to stay. She promised she would be quiet, respectful, and keep to herself, which was exactly what Lauren and Mark were hoping for. They welcomed her into their home, naively believing the arrangement would be simple and straightforward.

At first, everything seemed fine. Anna kept her distance, coming and going with a reserved politeness that never gave Lauren and Mark any reason to doubt her. She would often disappear for long hours, claiming to be busy with "research" or "meetings," leaving the house empty and still. But gradually, subtle shifts began to occur.

Lauren was the first to notice. It started with strange noises—soft murmurs, whispers—coming from Anna's room late at night. The walls were thin, but these sounds were not the usual noises of someone asleep. These were more deliberate, more... controlled. Occasionally, Lauren thought she heard faint clicks or whirrs—like the sound of machines being switched on and off.

When Mark noticed the unusual stains in the bathroom—a streak of something dark, something almost organic smeared on the floor—he assumed it was an accident, something Anna had carelessly left behind. But it was only when Lauren found a set of unfamiliar needles and syringes in the bathroom drawer that their unease deepened. They didn't confront Anna immediately. They didn't want to jump to conclusions, but the strange feeling of being watched, of being *aware* of something they couldn't quite place, grew each day.

The real horror came when Lauren discovered the truth.

One night, unable to sleep, she wandered the house, her mind whirling with questions. She couldn't shake the suspicion that Anna was hiding something—something far more sinister than a messy tenant. She tiptoed toward Anna's room, only to stop in her tracks when she noticed the faint glow of a light slipping out from under the door. Heart racing, she pressed her ear to the door.

Inside, Anna was talking softly, but the words didn't make sense. She wasn't speaking to anyone. The murmurs were like a ritual, a chant, an incantation. Something in Lauren's stomach turned as she listened. It wasn't just a conversation—it was something darker, something ritualistic. The silence that followed was broken only by the soft hum of a machine.

Lauren's breath caught in her throat as she turned the handle, the door creaking open just a crack.

What she saw sent ice through her veins.

Anna stood in the middle of the room, her back to the door, wearing a long, dark robe. Surrounding her were dozens of jars—glass containers filled with strange, unsettling contents. Some of the jars were filled with thick, viscous liquids, while others contained pieces of something too grotesque to identify. As Lauren's eyes scanned the room, she saw several monitors, each displaying digital readouts, numbers she couldn't understand, but that felt deeply wrong. In the corner of the room was a chair—a chair that looked like it belonged in a torture chamber—strapped with leather restraints.

On the desk in front of Anna lay a small, unconscious figure, their face obscured by shadows. A figure that was barely recognizable, someone in a deep sleep or unconscious state. The machine hummed louder now, as Anna injected something into the figure's arm.

Lauren's pulse thundered in her ears. She stumbled backward, her mind unable to process the horror unfolding before her. She wanted to run, to scream, but her legs were frozen. The door clicked shut behind her, and she was plunged back into darkness.

The next day, everything seemed normal—too normal. Anna was polite, as always, offering a smile and a friendly wave as she left for the day. But Lauren and Mark knew something had shifted. The atmosphere in the house felt heavy, suffocating, as though they were trapped inside a waking nightmare.

They found themselves increasingly paranoid, unable to shake the feeling that Anna knew they had seen too much. They tried to act normal, to maintain their routine, but the oppressive weight of the unknown pressed down on them. They could no longer escape the dark reality of what was happening in their own home.

One night, unable to bear the silence any longer, Mark followed Anna. He had to know what she was doing. His heart raced as he trailed her down the street, careful to keep his distance. When she finally stopped at a small, nondescript building on the edge of town, he watched from the shadows. He had no idea what was going on, but he knew it wasn't good. His eyes widened as he saw Anna enter the building, her face hidden behind a mask.

Suddenly, a sharp pain pierced Mark's chest. He turned around in time to see Anna standing there, her face twisted in a cold, knowing smile. She had been expecting him.

"You shouldn't have come, Mark," she said, her voice eerily calm. "Now you'll see."

Before he could react, the world around him began to spin. His body grew heavy, his mind clouded with confusion. The last thing he heard was Anna's voice, cold and detached.

"It was never about the rent," she murmured. "You were the experiment."

The following days were a blur. When Mark and Lauren woke up, they were back in their house, but everything felt wrong. The walls seemed to close in, and the air felt too thick, too suffocating. They couldn't remember how they had returned, but they could feel the weight of Anna's presence. It was like the house had become a cage, and they were trapped inside it, unable to escape the horrors that had unfolded within it.

Days passed, and they could hear strange noises in the night—the sounds of footsteps, whispered conversations, the hum of machines—sounds they couldn't escape. The realization set in that Anna's experiments weren't just confined to one person; they had become part of something far darker, something they couldn't fight. They were locked inside their own home, with nowhere to run, and Anna's twisted experiments would continue.

And in the quiet, oppressive darkness of the night, the house seemed to breathe—alive with the consequences of their own misguided kindness. The consequences of the shared economy had taken root, and there was no escape from the nightmare that had consumed them.

"The Tenant"

It was supposed to be a simple transaction—just a few weeks, an easy way to cover rent while they went home for winter break. Four college students, crammed into a small apartment, had never considered the consequences of renting out their space to a stranger. They had each found their own corners of the world to escape to for the holidays, leaving the apartment empty. To save on bills, they decided to list it online, offering it to travelers or anyone needing a place to stay. They didn't expect anything to come of it—just a little money to cover the rent.

But when they returned to the apartment weeks later, the atmosphere was different. The door creaked open, and an odd chill washed over them. The place was *too quiet*—the kind of silence that feels heavy, as if the air itself has become oppressive.

All four students felt it the moment they stepped through the door.

The apartment, once vibrant with their chaotic energy, was now sterile, unnervingly still. The living room was dim, shadows curling in the corners like they had been waiting for them. But it wasn't just the silence that unnerved them—it was the objects.

Strange objects.

They were scattered across the apartment, things that didn't belong, things they had never seen before. The most unsettling was a small, intricately carved wooden box sitting on the coffee table. It had no labels, no markings, just a faint glow that seemed to pulse with an unnatural rhythm, as if it were alive. Around the box were piles of photographs, some of which were clearly taken inside the apartment. The people in the photos were unfamiliar, their eyes wide with something like fear or confusion, faces blurred in a way that was impossible to describe. It felt like the images were watching them.

"What the hell is this?" Sam muttered, staring at the box with a mixture of curiosity and unease.

But it wasn't just the box. Objects were scattered throughout the apartment—random trinkets and tokens that felt wrong. The kitchen was lined with unfamiliar jars of herbs and powders, all labeled with cryptic symbols. A black-and-white photograph, faded with age, sat framed on the windowsill, showing a group of people in old-fashioned clothing, standing in front of a building that looked nothing like the apartment building. The scene in the photo felt disjointed, out of place, and the longer they stared at it, the more the faces seemed to twist into something unrecognizable.

"Okay, this is... not cool," Lily said, her voice tight with anxiety. "Did anyone leave this stuff here?"

None of them had. They all exchanged wary glances, but no one spoke. The tension in the room grew thick, palpable, as if the air itself was holding its breath.

That night, things began to happen. Small at first, like shadows flickering at the edge of their vision, darting across walls when no one was looking directly. Sam tried to shake it off, but the shadows seemed to grow bolder with each passing hour. He would look away for a second, only to find them longer, more solid, as if they were creeping closer to him. He tried to convince himself it was the stress from exams, the cold, or lack of sleep, but deep down, he knew that something was terribly wrong.

Lily was the first to hear it—whispers, faint and distant, echoing through the walls, muffled as if they were coming from the next room. But no one else seemed to hear them, and when she pointed it out to the others, they all shrugged it off. Yet that night, they too began to hear it—the soft murmurs, the indistinct voices, sometimes calling their names, other times murmuring in languages they couldn't understand. The sound seemed to surround them, pressing in from all directions, making it impossible to escape.

The following days blurred into a haze of anxiety. The visions started to become more intense. First, it was just glimpses—figures moving just out of their sight, or faces that would appear in the mirror only to disappear when they looked directly at them. But soon, the hallucinations became more vivid, more real. Sam would see shadows moving through the hallway when no one was there. Lily saw a figure standing in her doorway late one night—an older woman, her face obscured by long, black hair, her eyes empty hollows. When Lily reached out to touch her, the woman vanished in a puff of smoke.

The others weren't spared either. Mark saw the box—*the box*—glow faintly in the middle of the night, its pulse matching the beat of his heart. When he touched it, a violent jolt of energy coursed through him, sending him stumbling backward, his head spinning with visions of twisted shapes and symbols. He had to run from the room, the walls seeming to bend in on him.

The apartment itself began to feel like it was alive, its boundaries warping and shifting. The walls seemed to breathe, the floors creaking underfoot in ways they hadn't before. It was as though the place was watching them, suffocating them, closing in.

Desperation grew. They tried to leave, to get away from the apartment, but the moment they stepped out the door, the streets seemed wrong. They walked in circles, unable to leave the block, as if the world itself had become distorted. When they tried to call for help, their phones would freeze, the call dropping before they could reach anyone. It was like they were trapped in a loop, a prison built from the very walls of the apartment they had rented to a stranger.

And then, one night, as they stood in the living room, the door suddenly slammed shut. They rushed to the windows, but the view was no longer the one they knew. The street outside was gone. Instead, there was nothing but a deep, empty darkness stretching into infinity, as if the world had collapsed into some abyss.

It was then they realized the true horror. The tenant—the stranger they had let into their home—hadn't just left behind objects. She had left behind *a curse*. She had used the apartment for something far darker than they could have imagined. The objects were not just artifacts; they were vessels for something far older and malevolent. And now, they were trapped, unable to escape, forever bound to the consequences of their decision.

The last thing they heard was the whisper of the voices, clear and loud now, as if they were standing right next to them. But it wasn't just their names they whispered—it was a chant, an incantation, a summoning.

The walls closed in, and the shadows reached out, swallowing them whole.

"The Strangers in My Home"

At first, it felt like a perfect solution.

Tara, a young woman new to the city, had been struggling to make ends meet. After her apartment lease ended, she moved into a small, run-down unit in a building that reeked of old carpet and lost potential. It wasn't much, but it was cheap. When the idea of renting out her extra room to strangers crossed her mind, it seemed harmless. She had nothing valuable to hide—just a few belongings, a small bed, and the remnants of a life she had left behind in her old city.

It was a shared economy, after all. Everyone was doing it. She found a post on a popular rental platform, listing her room for a few hundred dollars a month, and before long, she had her first guest: Lucas. He was a quiet man, in his mid-thirties, polite but distant. He paid upfront, moved in, and hardly ever left the room. He never made much noise, just a few footsteps down the hall now and then. Tara figured he was either an introvert or just busy with work—no cause for concern.

A few weeks passed, and Lucas was followed by another guest—a couple named Diane and Michael, who seemed friendly but just as secretive. They too mostly kept to themselves. They were quiet, respectful, and after a couple of nights, Tara felt a sense of comfort in the routine of living with strangers. The money helped, and her space, though small, felt safer with the presence of others in it.

But that sense of safety began to erode with small, subtle shifts in the atmosphere.

The first incident happened one morning when Tara woke up to find her favorite bracelet—one she always left on her nightstand—was missing. At first, she thought she must have misplaced it, but as the days passed, more things began to disappear: her earrings, her phone charger, the spare change she kept in her wallet. It was easy to dismiss at first—after all, she was living with strangers. People misplaced things, right?

But it was the little things that gnawed at her.

Tara's sleep became increasingly disturbed. She would wake up with the unmistakable feeling that something was wrong—her room was colder than it should have been, or the sheets on her bed would be slightly shifted, as if someone had touched them while she was asleep. She began to notice odd things in the house: the front door left slightly ajar, the lights flickering when no one was around, and the unsettling feeling of being watched even when no one was there.

One night, she stayed up late working on her laptop. She was in the living room when she heard something—footsteps in the hallway, soft and deliberate. She looked up, her heart racing. It was late, too late for any of her roommates to be awake. But when she glanced down the hallway, the shadows were still. The house was silent.

Tara tried to brush it off, but it was harder and harder to ignore the feeling of unease creeping into every corner of the apartment. She started locking her bedroom door at night, but still, the small items kept disappearing. The jewelry she rarely wore was gone. Her credit card had been used for small, inexplicable charges. Tara confronted Lucas and the couple, but each of them denied any involvement, offering feigned looks of innocence. They were so convincing, so smooth, that Tara second-guessed herself.

But then, one evening, she stayed up late again, determined to get to the bottom of the strange happenings. She set up her phone to record the hallway, tucked under a pillow on the couch. And then, as she lay in bed, her pulse thundering in her ears, she waited.

It didn't take long.

In the dead of night, Tara's phone caught the shadows of movement—shapes slipping from door to door, quiet footsteps padding across the floor. She saw Lucas, his figure briefly illuminated by the faint light from the hallway, moving toward her room. Her heart raced as she watched him. He was holding something—a bag, bulky and heavy, moving carefully but quickly toward the living room. Then, Diane and Michael appeared, silent as they helped him load it.

Her phone caught it all—the silent thefts, the meticulous manner in which they removed things from every corner of the apartment, from her drawer where she kept her most personal belongings to the pantry where they took more than just food. It was not just items from her room—it was everything. The thieves were systematically clearing out every valuable thing they could find.

Tara's mind spun as she watched in horror. The people she had trusted, the strangers she had invited into her life, had been stealing from her for weeks. Every item was being taken with such cold precision. Her heart pounded in her chest, but she couldn't move, couldn't even scream. She was paralyzed, trapped in her own home, her sanctuary now violated.

As they finished their task and returned to their rooms, the shadows began to fade, and the apartment grew still once more. Tara didn't move for a long time, her body rigid with fear. She could hear her breath, shallow and quick, but the world felt far away, like she wasn't in it anymore.

She had been living with thieves. They had methodically picked apart her life while she slept, while she trusted them. Tara's worst fear had come true—the strangers she had shared her life with had become a force of terror she could no longer escape.

The next morning, she was ready to confront them. Her hands shook as she packed her things, but when she went into the living room, there was no sign of Lucas, Diane, or Michael. Their rooms were empty. They had vanished without a trace, leaving behind an apartment full of nothing but memories of a crime she couldn't undo. The lock on her door was still there, but now it felt like a hollow protection—useless, as though the invaders had always been inside, waiting for the moment to strike.

She stood in the empty apartment, her belongings scattered around her, and realized with a chilling certainty that she had been trapped from the start. The shared economy had been the perfect mask for their thievery, the perfect cover for the dark, twisted act that had played out under her nose. And now, there was nothing left to do but pick up the pieces of her life, to live with the creeping knowledge that trust could be shattered in an instant. The consequences of her decision to share her space had been irreversible.

There was no escape from the strangers she had invited into her home, and as the reality of what had happened settled over her, Tara realized that nothing would ever feel safe again.

"The Garden of Sins"

The Jeffersons were a family of simple means. Their small home, nestled at the edge of a quiet town, was surrounded by a lush, sprawling garden that had been passed down through generations. For years, it had been the family's pride—a sanctuary of fragrant flowers, well-tended vegetables, and a peaceful place to spend time. But times were tough, and the family was struggling. With rising bills and the weight of daily life pressing down on them, they had an idea that seemed harmless enough. They could rent out the space in their garden. A few extra dollars could ease the burden, and they never thought twice about the arrangement.

It was Michael, a man in his early forties, who had come to them with an unusual request. He was polite, charming even, with a calm demeanor that instantly made them feel at ease. He claimed to be a private researcher, someone studying the effects of nature on rare species, and he promised to keep his work discreet. The rent was more than fair, and in return, he'd tend to the garden, offering to cultivate some exotic plants for the family. He said he had "specialized knowledge" that could enhance the garden's growth. He would take care of the space, leaving everything in pristine condition when he was done.

At first, things seemed harmless enough. Michael arrived with his supplies, setting up small greenhouses, planting unusual seeds, and creating neat rows of plants and trees that seemed to grow faster than anything the family had ever seen. The flowers were brighter, the vegetables larger, and the plants thicker and more vibrant. The family marveled at the strange beauty of it all.

But then, strange things began to happen.

The air around the garden became thick, almost oppressive. At night, when the wind would blow, there were noises—soft clicking sounds, strange rustling in the underbrush that made the family uneasy. The once-pleasant scent of the garden began to change, replaced by a sour, acrid stench that lingered in the air. When they asked Michael about it, he would brush it off, claiming that the research required certain conditions. He assured them it was all part of his work, that everything was under control.

But it wasn't.

The first sign came when the family noticed a large, dark figure moving just beyond the garden fence. At first, they thought it was a stray animal—perhaps a large dog or a deer—but the shape didn't look right. It was too large, too unnatural. The following night, they heard something else—scratching at the window, a soft tapping sound as if claws were dragging across the glass. Terrified, they went outside to investigate, but there was nothing there. Just the shadows of the garden, stretching unnaturally in the moonlight.

Days later, things began to disappear—small animals, pets that had wandered too close to the garden. The Jeffersons' cat, Whiskers, was the first to go. The family scoured the neighborhood, called animal shelters, and posted flyers, but there was no trace of him. The air grew thicker, the garden darker, as if something sinister had taken root within it.

One evening, while Michael was away, the family decided to take a closer look at the garden themselves. They had been growing more suspicious, and their unease had turned into palpable dread. When they ventured into the heart of the garden, they were struck by the sight of something unnatural—a massive, gnarled tree at the center of the plot, its branches twisted into grotesque shapes. Underneath it, the ground was damp and slick with a thick, black substance. And there, scattered around the roots, were the remains of small animals—rabbits, squirrels, birds—all torn apart, their bodies mangled and discarded like refuse.

A sudden movement caught their eye. Something large and scaled was slithering from beneath the underbrush. It was a creature unlike anything they had ever seen—its body long, serpentine, covered in glistening black scales that shimmered in the dim light. Its eyes were wide, black, and empty, and its fangs were sharp, glistening with venom. The family screamed and ran inside, slamming the door behind them.

That night, they sat huddled together, fear creeping into their bones as they realized the truth. Michael had turned their peaceful garden into a breeding ground for monstrous, deadly creatures—beasts of nightmare that were no longer bound by the natural order. The garden was no longer a sanctuary; it was a trap, a place of death.

When Michael returned the next morning, his face was pale, his eyes too calm. He walked into the house as if nothing were amiss, offering them a smile that made their skin crawl.

"Everything is progressing as expected," he said, his voice too soft, too controlled. "The species I've been cultivating are more resilient, more powerful than I thought. Your garden is thriving in ways you couldn't have imagined."

Tara, the mother, couldn't hold back any longer. "What the hell have you done to our garden? What *are* those things?"

Michael's eyes glinted with a hint of something darker. "Don't worry. They'll be gone soon. I just needed the right conditions, the right... environment to grow them. You've done your part."

The room went cold, and Tara's stomach churned as she realized the horrifying truth. They weren't just part of his research—they were part of *his experiment*. The Jeffersons had unknowingly been complicit in his twisted breeding program, unwittingly fostering deadly creatures in their very own backyard.

But it was too late to stop it now.

The creatures were multiplying, growing faster, becoming more aggressive with each passing hour. The air thickened with the scent of decay, and the ground trembled as something large and monstrous began to emerge from the depths of the garden. The Jeffersons tried to flee, but the garden had become their prison. The creatures were everywhere now, lurking in the shadows, their eyes gleaming in the darkness.

As the family desperately tried to escape, the garden seemed to swallow them whole, the plants and trees growing more alive, more insidious, closing in around them. Every door was blocked, every window covered with vines and thorns, the creatures pressing against the walls, waiting for their moment to strike.

When Michael left, he left them with a nightmare they could never escape.

The family was trapped, forced to fight for their lives against the monsters that had been born from their own foolishness. The garden—once a place of peace, a small refuge from the world—had become a breeding ground for horror. There was no way out. No way to undo what had been done.

And in the suffocating darkness of the garden, with creatures lurking just beyond the walls, the Jeffersons realized the full extent of their mistake: the shared economy had cost them everything.

"The Photographer's Lens"

The Collins family was just trying to make ends meet. After months of tightening their belts, they decided to rent out their home while they went on vacation. The idea was simple: put up a listing online, let someone stay in their place for a few weeks, and in return, make some extra money. It was supposed to be easy—nothing more than a temporary arrangement, a small concession to the rising cost of living.

Enter Victor, the photographer.

He came across as polite, well-spoken, and a little eccentric, but nothing that would set off alarm bells. He said he was looking for a quiet place to stay while working on a personal project. He didn't mind that the house wasn't the grandest—just that it had "character," he told them. Victor paid upfront, a tidy sum for the month, and promised to treat the house with respect. His references were flawless. He had no reason to doubt him. The Collins family packed their bags and left, eager to escape their everyday struggles for a while.

But when they returned, the house they knew—the house they had called home—was different. The air felt thick, suffocating, as though something had taken root in every corner. They didn't notice it immediately. At first, it just felt... off. Like when you walk into a room and feel someone's presence even though they aren't there. An odd weight to the silence, an unnatural stillness.

The smell hit them first—stale, metallic, almost sweet, like rotting flowers. They assumed it was just the lingering smell of cleaning supplies, something left behind by Victor, but as they moved through the house, it became clear that there was something else entirely.

Lena, the mother, went into the living room to drop off her suitcase, and froze. On the wall was a photograph—a huge, grainy portrait of her, her face twisted in an expression of terror, her eyes wide and glassy. She didn't recognize the moment the photo had been taken, but it was unmistakably her. *Her.* And worse yet, her likeness was distorted, as though manipulated by some dark, unseen hand. The shadows in the image seemed to wrap around her like suffocating hands.

Frozen, she stumbled backward, her heart pounding. The room felt smaller, more oppressive. Her breath caught as she noticed more photographs lining the walls, and it wasn't just her—there were images of her husband, Greg, her children, Jason and Sophie, all twisted, contorted, and dehumanized. Faces stretched in agony, limbs distorted, as if captured in moments of intense pain or fear. They were *their* faces, their likenesses, but there was no trace of the people they were. They had become grotesque caricatures of themselves, trapped in a twisted, horrifying version of reality.

"Greg... Greg, come here," she whispered, her voice trembling.

Greg came running, his face full of concern as he saw her standing in the living room, staring at the wall in horror. He followed her gaze, and his face fell as he took in the photographs, the sickening images that now adorned their home.

"This... this isn't possible," Greg muttered, his voice a mix of disbelief and revulsion. "He—he took these while we were gone? How?"

Lena moved toward the other side of the room, her heart racing. As she approached the kitchen, she noticed a strange, almost imperceptible sound, a soft humming, like a machine running in the background. Her eyes narrowed as she looked toward the table, where another set of photographs were neatly laid out—larger, darker, more unsettling. But these weren't just photographs. They were prints, stretched across the table, and the faces on them were not just distorted—they were *altered*. Sections of the photographs had been violently cut out and replaced with images of dead animals, twisted human figures, and abstract forms that sent a shiver crawling down her spine.

Her skin prickled with dread. There was something so intimately wrong about it. It wasn't just the images. It was the *intent*. The way these images were meant to convey something grotesque, something dehumanizing.

Lena felt the walls closing in. The air in the house felt too thick, the shadows too alive. As she backed away from the table, her foot caught something soft—a rolled-up piece of fabric. She turned and found an old coat, draped in the corner. She lifted it, horrified to find it covered in patches of bloodstained cloth and what looked like scraps of human hair.

Then, the realization hit her like a crushing wave.

Victor hadn't just stayed in their home. He had *used* it. He had used *them*—the Collins family—*as subjects* for his sick, macabre art. He had made them the centerpiece of his twisted project. This wasn't just photography. This was *creation*, but creation of the most vile kind. He had transformed their home into a sinister set, a stage where their lives were turned into something unrecognizable, something grotesque.

Greg's voice broke through her thoughts. "Lena... look at this."

He was standing at the back door, his hand trembling as he held up a roll of film. The film had been exposed, but it wasn't film at all. It was strips of some kind of *tape*, each frame revealing moments of the family's life—laughing around the dinner table, reading books in the living room, playing with their dog—except these moments weren't captured by a lens. They had been *staged*. Someone had been there—watching, waiting, setting up every scene with the intention of twisting it into something horrifying.

As Greg turned to face Lena, his eyes wild with panic, the lights flickered. The house seemed to pulse with an unnatural energy. The walls groaned and shifted, and the floor beneath them seemed to vibrate with an unseen force. Lena could almost hear the whisper of the camera shutter—the mechanical, cold sound of Victor's lens capturing their likenesses in ways that could never be erased.

Suddenly, the house didn't feel like home anymore. It felt like a tomb. A tomb where they were trapped, where their lives had been turned into art—into a grotesque tableau they could never escape.

The terror settled in their bones as they heard the unmistakable sound of footsteps in the attic. Slowly, they turned toward the stairs, their hearts racing. They weren't alone anymore. Victor had left his mark, and now, they were his captives, his creations, trapped in a house that no longer resembled the place they once knew.

With every step they took toward the attic, the walls seemed to close in tighter. Every corner, every shadow was filled with the specter of Victor's twisted art, and the terrible truth settled in their hearts—there was no escape from the consequences of their decision. Their home had become a canvas for the horrors of the shared economy, and now they had to face the nightmare that had been born inside it.

"The Cursed Stay"

Clara and James had always been the type of couple who believed in the goodness of people. Their quaint cottage, tucked away in a quiet neighborhood just on the outskirts of the city, was their pride. After years of hard work, they had finally purchased the place, and they couldn't wait to share it with others. It was a peaceful, charming home—filled with light from the large windows, a crackling fireplace in the living room, and a garden blooming with vibrant flowers. They loved the idea of renting out their space to tourists, letting others enjoy the beauty of their home while making a little extra income to help pay the mortgage.

It seemed like an innocent enough idea—just renting out their spare room to travelers passing through. At first, their guests were friendly, respectful, and easy to please. The arrangement worked perfectly, and Clara and James were pleased with the extra cash it brought in. But then came Victor.

Victor was a quiet, introverted man in his late thirties, with dark, intense eyes that seemed to look past people instead of at them. He was polite enough, but there was something about him that made Clara feel uneasy. He had a particular way of speaking, slow and deliberate, as though each word was carefully considered. His presence in their home was always calm, but it felt like there was something lurking beneath the surface—something hidden behind his stoic demeanor.

At first, everything seemed fine. Victor stayed mostly to himself, leaving early in the mornings and returning late at night. He occasionally wandered the garden, taking pictures of the flowers and trees, but nothing out of the ordinary stood out. Yet after he left, Clara and James started to notice something unsettling.

The first sign came in the living room. A strange mark appeared on the wall, just beside the fireplace. It was faint, at first, but clear enough to make Clara pause. It looked like a symbol, a series of angular lines intersecting with one another. James shrugged it off, thinking it was just dirt or perhaps something that had come off Victor's bag or clothing. But when they tried to clean it, the mark wouldn't come off. It remained, faint but persistent, as if the wall itself had been branded.

Then, the noises started.

It began with soft whispers in the night. Low, unintelligible voices that seemed to drift through the walls. Clara woke in the dead of night, her heart pounding, only to lie still and listen. At first, she thought it was just the wind, or perhaps an animal outside. But no—this was different. The voices were too clear, too purposeful. They came from inside the house, from somewhere deep within the walls.

James, too, began to hear things. Scratching at the windows when no one was outside. Faint footsteps on the staircase when no one was upstairs. It became impossible to ignore. They'd hear things in the house, but when they investigated, there was no one there. Every corner seemed to hold shadows that weren't there before. Every room felt heavier, as though something unseen was pressing in, waiting.

Clara, growing more paranoid with each passing day, began to examine the house more closely. She noticed that the strange symbol that had appeared on the wall wasn't just an isolated incident. It was showing up in other places—in the corners of windows, etched into the backs of chairs, carved into the old wood of the floors. Small, disturbing marks, symbols that were impossible to ignore. They felt... wrong.

When Clara finally took the time to research them, her stomach dropped. The symbols were not just random markings. They were part of an ancient occult script, associated with old curses and dark rituals. She couldn't remember exactly what they meant, but the feeling of dread that filled her chest was enough to make her heart race.

James dismissed her concerns at first, but as the weeks passed, the atmosphere in the house became more suffocating. The whispers grew louder. The shadows in the corners of the rooms stretched longer, darker. And worst of all, they began to feel watched. Every time they turned a corner, there was a feeling of something—someone—just out of view, lurking just beyond their sight.

The air itself seemed to thicken, the walls pressing in on them. Even the light felt different—too dim, too heavy, as though the very essence of the house had been tainted. The house was no longer a sanctuary. It was a prison.

One night, Clara and James sat in the living room, trying to distract themselves from the growing sense of unease. They had closed all the curtains, locked the doors, and tried to make the house feel normal again. But nothing could erase the feeling that they were not alone.

That's when they heard it—the unmistakable sound of something scraping against the floorboards. A slow, deliberate dragging sound. It came from upstairs. Clara's breath caught in her throat as the sound grew louder, moving closer.

They both stood in frozen terror. The temperature dropped, the air growing cold around them. Then, without warning, the lights flickered and went out. A heavy silence filled the house.

Clara grabbed James' hand, pulling him toward the stairs. "We have to check," she whispered, but the words didn't feel like they came from her. The voice was no longer her own. It was as if the house itself was speaking through her.

The moment they reached the top of the stairs, the door to the spare room—the one they had rented to Victor—swung open by itself, creaking on its hinges. The room inside was empty, but the air was thick with a presence that made Clara's skin crawl.

On the floor, a fresh symbol was scrawled, smeared with something dark and sticky—blood.

The room felt alive, as if the walls were closing in, suffocating them. They couldn't breathe. The weight of the house was too much. The whispers grew louder, more urgent. The darkness in the corners seemed to rise up and move toward them, wrapping around them like tendrils.

They tried to leave, to escape, but the house wouldn't let them. The door slammed shut with a violent force, and the walls seemed to shift, trapping them inside. The house had become a cage, and they were its prey.

In the end, they realized the truth too late. Victor had not just stayed in their home—he had left behind something far worse than they could have imagined. The symbols, the rituals, had brought a curse upon the house, one that could not be undone. Their decision to share their home, to open the door to a stranger, had turned their sanctuary into a nightmare.

The last thing they saw was the shadows closing in, the whispers filling their ears, and the unmistakable sense that they were no longer alone in the house.

"The Artist's Touch"

Ellie had always been a pragmatic woman. A small business owner, she rented out her studio space to artists, offering an affordable place for creative individuals to hone their craft. Over the years, she'd met all sorts of tenants—painters, sculptors, photographers—each one a bit quirky but harmless, each one leaving her studio with their work, nothing more than a fleeting presence in her life. So when Max, an artist who specialized in body modifications, came to her with an offer to rent the space for a few months, Ellie didn't think twice. He was well-spoken, charming in a way that made him seem like someone who had a deep understanding of art. He claimed he was working on a series of "experimental pieces" and promised to keep the noise down. The rent was good, and Max was polite enough to make Ellie feel comfortable with the idea.

She wasn't worried about his craft. She'd heard of body modifications before—piercings, tattoos, the occasional branding—but nothing that would suggest this project was anything out of the ordinary. The work was still considered "art," after all, pushing the boundaries of aesthetics and form. Ellie was open-minded; she understood the need for space in which to create. She didn't question it. She was just happy to have a steady tenant.

At first, everything seemed normal. Max would come and go, carrying strange medical-looking equipment, sometimes dragging a large duffel bag full of supplies, which Ellie assumed were for his art. He worked late into the night, often keeping to himself, but the studio was always locked up when he left, the key returned neatly to the mailbox. He didn't socialize much, and Ellie didn't mind that. He was quiet, he paid on time, and there were no complaints.

But then, Ellie started noticing changes in the studio's appearance.

The walls, once clean and white, now had faint smudges, streaks of something dark, that seemed to stain them in patterns she couldn't quite decipher. She initially thought it was just dust or dirt, perhaps from the heavy equipment Max was using. But there was something about the way it marked the walls—an unsettling symmetry in the stains, almost deliberate. Then, there were the strange tools left lying around: sharp blades, surgical scissors, scalpels, and needles. She'd see them on the counter when she came to check on the studio, carefully set down and neatly arranged, as though to suggest Max had been meticulous. But the sheer volume of equipment unnerved her.

She didn't dare ask Max about it. After all, it was his art, his project.

Then came the night she couldn't ignore it anymore.

It was well past midnight when Ellie decided to visit the studio. She had just returned from a late meeting, and her curiosity had gotten the better of her. She had always been slightly unsettled by the dark, mysterious atmosphere Max carried around him, but tonight, she could no longer shake the feeling that something wasn't right. She tried to open the door to the studio, but it was locked. It wasn't unusual for Max to lock the door when he was working late, but this time, Ellie's instincts told her that something was off.

She stood there for a moment, listening to the silence that hung thick in the air. Then, she heard a noise—faint but unmistakable—the sound of something being scraped across the floor. Ellie's breath hitched in her throat. She had heard that sound before, somewhere deep in her memory, but couldn't place it. The feeling of dread gnawed at her. She knocked on the door softly, but there was no response. She knocked harder, her hand trembling. After a long pause, she heard footsteps, slow and measured, moving toward the door.

When Max opened it, he was smiling, his face pale under the harsh light, his eyes wide with an intensity that unnerved Ellie. His lab coat was stained with something dark, something that glistened faintly in the light. Ellie didn't ask him what had happened. She didn't need to. She could feel it—the terror hanging in the air.

"What's going on in there, Max?" she asked, her voice strained.

Max's smile widened, too wide, too strange. "Just some new work. I've been experimenting. You wouldn't understand."

Ellie felt the blood drain from her face as she stepped inside. Her eyes scanned the room. The scent hit her first—something metallic, like iron—but deeper, more visceral. The walls, once pristine, were now marred with disturbing drawings, sketches of human anatomy, body parts, muscles, veins—dissections laid out with clinical precision. But it wasn't just the drawings. It was the mannequins, too—lifelike, human-shaped forms that were missing limbs, their faces contorted in horror, their skin sewn together in unnatural patterns. It was as if Max had taken his "art" too far, pushed it beyond the realm of mere body modification into something dark, grotesque, and inhumane.

Max stepped closer, his voice low, almost soothing. "I wanted to take it further, Ellie. I needed the right canvas. The human body... it's beautiful in its raw form, but it's fragile, isn't it? I've been perfecting it, testing new techniques. I wanted to see how much it could endure."

Ellie's legs went weak. She backed away from him, her heart hammering. "You've been experimenting... on people?"

Max's eyes glinted. "Yes, but not just any people. Volunteers. They came to me, Ellie. Willing. They wanted to be a part of something special, something transformative. And I gave them what they wanted."

Ellie felt bile rise in her throat as she looked at the unfinished figures on the table, grotesque patches of skin, open wounds where muscle tissue had been exposed, discolored flesh. These were no longer human. They were... experiments.

It was then that she noticed the small figure in the corner of the room, barely covered by a blood-stained sheet. Her breath caught in her throat as she took a step closer, horrified by the shape beneath. And as the sheet was pulled away, she recoiled, her scream caught in her throat.

The figure on the table was once a person. Now, it was an abomination, a twisted mockery of a human being. The eyes were sewn shut, the mouth stretched wide open in a grotesque, eternal scream, and the limbs—distorted, unnaturally long, broken, and reattached in places they shouldn't be. It was still breathing, though labored, as if trying to scream, as if trying to escape—but it couldn't.

Max stepped behind her, his voice smooth, almost reverent. "It's beautiful, isn't it? It's not just modification. It's transcendence. I've taken the human form, and I've elevated it. I've pushed it beyond its limits, beyond what anyone else could imagine. This... this is what I've been creating."

Ellie couldn't breathe. The air had thickened to a suffocating pressure around her. The walls seemed to close in as she tried to escape, to run, but her legs refused to move.

Max laughed softly. "Don't be afraid, Ellie. You'll understand soon enough. You're part of this now, too."

Her blood ran cold as she turned and saw him holding a scalpel, his eyes wide and gleaming with that same twisted, maddening fervor. He stepped closer, his voice a whisper in her ear. "You'll be my next masterpiece."

The last thing Ellie heard before everything went dark was Max's voice, echoing through the studio, "It's beautiful. Just beautiful."

"The Unit"

When Tom first rented out the storage unit to Vincent, he thought it was a harmless business transaction. After all, Tom had been running his small, local storage facility for years, and his customers were usually nothing more than brief visitors—people needing a place to store some boxes, old furniture, or seasonal items. The business had always been simple, reliable. It was a way to make ends meet.

Vincent was different, though. From the start, there was something odd about him. He was polite, yes, but he was a man of few words. His movements were stiff, deliberate. He seemed to avoid eye contact, always glancing over his shoulder as if he were worried about someone seeing him. But Tom didn't ask questions. He just rented the unit out, and Vincent paid upfront for six months in advance. That was good for business, so Tom didn't push for details.

Over the next few weeks, Vincent came and went at odd hours, usually at night when the storage facility was closed. He'd arrive in an unmarked van, unload his things quickly, and disappear just as fast. Tom barely ever saw him, but he didn't mind. It wasn't unusual for customers to have odd schedules.

But soon, strange things started happening. The air around the storage unit, where Vincent's van was always parked, started to feel thick and sour. It was subtle at first—a faint, musty smell that lingered in the air, almost like rotting meat. Tom dismissed it as the smell of old cardboard or mildew, a normal part of running a facility with old buildings. But then it grew stronger.

One evening, after closing up the facility for the night, Tom locked up his office and stepped outside, only to notice that Vincent's van was parked in front of the unit again. This time, the door was slightly ajar, and Tom could see a dark shape moving inside. His gut tightened. There was something wrong about this, something that made the hairs on the back of his neck stand up.

He didn't know why, but he felt compelled to investigate. His mind raced with uneasy thoughts—what was Vincent hiding? The sounds, the strange smell—it was all too much. So, with a cautious step, he approached the storage unit.

The door creaked open. The smell hit him like a punch to the stomach—thick, cloying, suffocating. It was unbearable, and it took all his willpower not to gag as he peered inside.

What he saw made his heart skip a beat.

Inside the dimly lit unit, the floor was covered in plastic sheeting—soaked in dark stains. Boxes and bags were stacked haphazardly, and there were strange objects piled around the edges. But what really sent a shiver down Tom's spine was the heavy, metallic smell in the air. He stepped inside, and his foot hit something soft. He looked down and saw a large duffel bag lying on the floor, its zipper slightly open. His hands trembled as he reached for it, pulling the zipper back with a sickeningly quiet sound. Inside, there was a body.

The figure was half-covered, wrapped in plastic, but it was unmistakable—an unnatural pale color, limbs twisted in ways they shouldn't be. Tom recoiled, the world around him spinning as he stumbled back.

His mind raced as he stumbled backward into the unit's cold concrete walls. What the hell had he gotten himself into?

As Tom's eyes scanned the unit, he noticed more bodies—stacked under blankets, hidden in crates, suffocated under old tarps. They were all the same—human, lifeless, and grotesque. Panic surged through him, and his breath quickened as the horrific reality set in: Vincent wasn't just hiding things—he was hiding *people*.

Suddenly, he heard the sound of footsteps outside the unit. Tom's heart slammed in his chest as he quickly stepped behind a stack of boxes, barely breathing, praying Vincent hadn't seen him. His hands were slick with sweat as he tried to make himself as small as possible, his mind racing with fear.

Vincent's figure appeared in the doorway, his back turned, unaware that Tom was inside. He carried something heavy in his arms, but Tom couldn't make out what it was in the dim light. The man moved methodically, as if this was a routine—an evil, sickening routine that Tom now understood all too well.

When Vincent set the new body down among the others, he turned to the stack of boxes, and Tom heard the unmistakable sound of a knife being drawn. It was like the blade was whispering through the air, cutting through the tension, sealing Tom's fate.

Vincent muttered to himself, an almost soothing whisper as he began cutting at the plastic wrapping of the body. Tom couldn't move. He couldn't speak. He couldn't breathe. Every part of him screamed for him to run, to escape—but his legs wouldn't obey.

And then, Vincent spoke.

"You should've stayed away," he said, his voice chillingly calm. "But now you're part of this, too."

The words hit Tom like a slap to the face. He wasn't just a bystander. He wasn't just a witness. He was complicit now. His feet moved before his mind could catch up, and in a blind panic, he bolted from the unit.

The metal door slammed behind him with a deafening bang.

But as Tom turned to run, he realized something worse: the gate was locked. The whole facility, the whole yard, was surrounded by a high metal fence. He couldn't leave. He was trapped.

He whirled around in desperation, but the facility seemed different. The walls loomed taller, closer. The shadows around him felt darker. The air had thickened. Vincent was no longer in the unit, but the silence was worse than his presence.

Then, Tom saw them. The bodies—their dead eyes now wide open, staring at him, watching him, following his every movement. They were no longer just in the unit. No, somehow, they were here with him. The air hummed with a malevolent force. The faces on the bodies were twisted in unimaginable pain, mouths frozen in screams of agony, eyes locked in a silent plea.

Tom ran. His breath was ragged, his legs numb, but he couldn't escape. He reached the gate and tried to climb over it, but his hands slipped, his fingers unable to grip the bars. As he struggled, he felt something cold and wet press against his back. He turned slowly, and there was Vincent, standing just a few feet away, a twisted smile on his face.

"You can't leave," he whispered, his voice soft but carrying an unbearable weight. "You're one of them now."

Tom's body froze. His hands trembled as he looked around at the horror that surrounded him. The facility had become a prison, a graveyard of monstrous secrets, and there was no escape.

In the end, Tom's worst fear was realized—he was not just a witness to the horror. He was part of it. The shared economy had brought him into this nightmare, and now there was no escaping the consequences. The bodies, the suffering, the terror—it had all become a part of him.

And in the dark silence of the storage unit, where the air was thick with death and despair, Tom realized there was no longer any way out. The cage was set. The door was closed. And they were all part of something much darker than they could have ever imagined.

"The Watcher"

When Lily first met Mark, she didn't think twice. She was a freelance graphic designer, working long hours from her small apartment in the city. She'd advertised the spare room for rent, hoping to offset some of her mounting bills. Mark's response came quickly. He seemed like a perfect fit—polite, friendly, and clean. He didn't ask for much, just a place to stay for a while. They met for coffee to discuss the details, and Lily was immediately taken by how comfortable he made her feel. He was a bit quiet, but kind, with a warm smile that always seemed to reach his eyes.

At first, everything was fine. Mark settled in quietly, always keeping to himself, coming and going at odd hours, like most people in the city. He seemed to enjoy the peace and solitude, something Lily appreciated. She didn't mind sharing her space. They occasionally had dinner together, chatting about life and work, but there was never any pressure. She started to feel at ease around him, and slowly, the apartment felt like it was becoming home again.

But then, little things started to change.

Lily noticed, for example, that her personal items began to shift around. The notebook she'd left on the kitchen counter would suddenly be on her bed. The book she was reading—always carefully marked with a bookmark—was now open, pages turned to a specific chapter. At first, she thought she was simply forgetting things. It was easy to blame stress, late nights, and the scattered nature of her work.

Then, there were the gifts.

It started innocuously enough—flowers, a small potted plant, a candle. But they weren't just any flowers. They were always her favorite types—the ones she had mentioned only once in passing, in an offhand comment. And the plant, a rare type she'd mentioned as being too expensive to buy for herself, appeared on her windowsill one day, as if out of nowhere. She thanked him at first, thinking it was sweet, thoughtful. But the gifts kept coming, becoming more personal, more unsettling. A vintage photograph of a woman, dressed like her, smiling in the exact same pose Lily had been caught in during one of their dinners. A notebook with her initials engraved on it, her handwriting already inside.

Lily's unease began to grow. It wasn't just the gifts. It was the feeling that Mark was always there—always in the background, watching. It wasn't until she came home one evening after a late meeting and found him sitting in the living room, staring at her laptop screen, that the dread began to settle in.

"I was just looking at your designs," he said, his voice calm, his eyes fixed on the screen as if nothing was amiss.

Lily froze. "You... you were looking through my work?"

"I hope that's okay. I really like your style."

It felt harmless enough on the surface, but something about the way he said it—too nonchalant, too casual—set off a deep, uneasy feeling in her stomach. She forced a smile, trying to hide the rising panic. "Sure, just... don't go into my private files, okay?"

But over the following days, things only became more uncomfortable. Lily would come home to find the apartment slightly different—furniture moved just an inch to the left, her coat on the hook when she was sure she had left it on the chair. The biggest shock came when she walked into her bedroom one evening and noticed a camera hidden behind a decorative vase on her shelf.

She froze.

Her heartbeat quickened as she stared at the small, inconspicuous lens, its red light blinking steadily. She could feel the blood drain from her face. *He's been watching me.*

Panicked, she confronted him that night. "Mark, I found a camera in my room," she said, her voice shaking.

Mark didn't seem startled. His face was still, calm, as if he'd been expecting the question. "It's just for security," he said, his smile widening slightly. "I thought you'd feel safer. You're not always here, and I wanted to make sure the apartment was protected."

Lily didn't know what to say. Her stomach churned. "Mark, you don't get to decide what's safe for me. Take it down. Now."

He didn't immediately respond. He just looked at her, his eyes darkening with an unsettling calm. "I'm just trying to take care of you, Lily. You never know who you can trust. I just want to make sure nothing happens to you."

Something about his words sent a cold shiver down her spine. She didn't trust him anymore. She demanded he remove the camera and leave, but his expression was unreadable, his gaze almost pitying. He agreed too easily.

The next few days were filled with an oppressive silence. Lily tried to go on as normal, but she couldn't shake the feeling that she was being watched, even when she was alone. She started to notice more cameras—hidden in plain sight now, behind paintings, tucked inside the clock on the wall. It was as if the apartment had become a maze, a labyrinth of eyes and lenses. Every time she turned around, there was another hidden camera, watching her every move.

She stopped locking the door at night, certain he could get in without her noticing. Her own apartment had become a prison.

Lily began to fear the gifts more than the cameras. Each one felt like a trap, a subtle manipulation. He was learning more about her with every present, every piece of information he gleaned. She was terrified of what he might do next.

And then, one day, she found the letter. It was in her desk drawer, hidden beneath a pile of bills. The envelope was sealed with wax, her name written in his neat handwriting. Inside, the letter was unsettlingly simple, yet it sent a wave of horror over her:

"I've been watching you for a long time, Lily. I know your every move, your every thought. Soon, you'll understand that this is where you belong. I will take care of you—everything you need, everything you desire. You just have to let me."

Her body trembled as she read the words, the feeling of suffocation growing thicker, tighter around her. She wanted to leave, to run, but she realized with a sickening clarity that she couldn't. He had already infiltrated every part of her life. The walls of her own apartment felt too close, the air too thick with his presence.

That night, after another long, sleepless evening, Lily found herself standing in the kitchen, staring at the knife drawer. She had never felt so powerless in her own home. It was as though the apartment, once a place of comfort, had become a cage. She was trapped, and every decision she made, every step she took, was watched by those cold, unblinking cameras.

Lily knew she couldn't stay, but she couldn't leave.

The terror that once resided only in the shadows now wrapped around her like a choking embrace, and as the room seemed to close in around her, she realized that Mark wasn't just a tenant. He was the *watcher*, and she had no escape.

"The Bet"

The Parker family had always prided themselves on being open and helpful. After years of struggling financially, they'd finally settled into a quiet, comfortable home in the suburbs. The house was small, but it was theirs, and the large garage at the back seemed perfect for a little extra income. When they listed it for rent, they didn't expect much. Maybe someone needed space to store boxes, or a car, or some tools. It was just a means to cover the rising utility bills.

It was George who first inquired about renting the garage. He seemed perfectly ordinary—quiet, polite, with a well-groomed beard and a sharp, professional air. His only request was for some privacy, as he wanted to use the space for his "business," which he didn't specify in detail. George offered to pay several months' rent upfront, and the Parkers, eager for the money, agreed without hesitation.

At first, everything seemed fine. George came and went at odd hours but always kept to himself. The garage door was always shut when the family was home, and no one ever heard anything unusual. The family even assumed George must be running some sort of small business—perhaps a part-time woodworking project or storage for his supplies.

But soon, things began to change.

It started subtly—small things at first. Unusual cars would appear on their street at night, parked near the garage, their headlights cutting through the dark, casting long shadows across the driveway. The family didn't think much of it. After all, George was an adult, and the house was his to use.

But then came the sound. Every night, when the Parkers were trying to sleep, they began to hear the faint hum of voices coming from the garage. Low murmurs, as if a crowd of people were gathered just on the other side of the wall. At first, they assumed George was hosting gatherings or meetings, but the laughter and noise were always too intense, too unsettling.

One evening, unable to ignore the gnawing feeling that something was wrong, Lisa, the matriarch of the family, decided to investigate. She crept down the hallway, trying to stay quiet, and stood by the kitchen window, which overlooked the garage. Through the small crack in the blinds, she saw something that made her blood run cold.

A group of men, their faces shadowed by the darkness, were gathered around a table in the garage, surrounded by piles of cash and stacks of chips. A single light hung above the table, casting harsh shadows on the walls. Lisa watched in stunned silence as the men shouted, slapped the table in excitement, and exchanged money in hurried, furtive movements.

It didn't take long for her to realize the truth: George wasn't just using the garage for storage. He was running an illegal gambling operation right under their noses.

Her heart pounded in her chest as she backed away from the window, her breath shallow. This wasn't a harmless mistake. This wasn't a couple of guys playing poker on a Friday night. This was something darker, something that could bring trouble into their lives.

Lisa tried to ignore it, hoping that it would all blow over. She didn't confront George immediately. But the noise, the cars, the tension—it all continued, growing every night until it became impossible to ignore. The gambling was no longer a side business—it was an operation, and it was getting out of control.

Then came the moment when everything changed.

One evening, Lisa and her husband, Tom, sat in the living room, trying to unwind after a long day, when they heard loud banging on the door. Their hearts skipped a beat. It was late, too late for anyone to be visiting. Tom cautiously opened the door to find two men standing on the porch. They were tall, their faces hard, and they were dressed in black jackets with no markings. No logos. Just intimidation.

"We're here to see George," one of them said, his voice low and threatening. "Is he home?"

Tom's pulse raced. "Uh, he's in the garage. What do you want with him?"

The man's eyes narrowed, and he smiled, though there was nothing kind in it. "Just tell him his friends are here for a chat."

The door slammed shut behind Tom as the men pushed past him, entering the house with a presence that made everything feel suffocating. They walked straight into the garage without waiting for permission. Tom's heart pounded in his chest as he turned to Lisa, fear flooding his every thought. Something was wrong. He knew it instinctively.

In the garage, the noise stopped suddenly—too abruptly. There was no sound of chips clattering or men shouting, just a deep, unnatural silence that pressed against the house. The minutes dragged on in agonizing quiet.

Then, everything happened in a rush.

The door to the garage burst open, and George stumbled out, his face pale, his shirt ripped, his body bloodied. He tried to move toward the front door, but two of the men grabbed him, throwing him against the wall, and one of them pulled out a knife. Tom stood frozen, horror-stricken, as George's voice cracked. "Please, no. I'm sorry, I didn't—"

But his words were cut off by the man's cold laugh.

"They don't *apologize*, George," the man said, voice like gravel. "Not when they *owe*."

Lisa screamed as the man turned toward her, his eyes gleaming with cold malice. The others moved toward Tom, their presence so overpowering that it felt like the walls were closing in. The room spun around him as he realized what they were here for: George had crossed someone. And now, they were going to make him pay.

The violence escalated. They shoved Tom to the ground, demanding money, threats in every word. The house was no longer a place of safety. It had become a battleground—a cage where a simple decision to rent out their garage had led them into the clutches of dangerous criminals.

As the men held them at gunpoint, and the sound of violence erupted in the garage, the full weight of the situation settled on the Parkers. They were trapped in their own home. Their life, their sanctuary, had been turned into a hell because of a simple mistake, a careless choice to trust a stranger.

By the time the men left, the damage had been done. They were gone, but the violence they'd brought lingered. George was gone, his fate sealed, but the terror had only just begun. The police wouldn't come—they'd never be able to trace what happened here. The gambling den was a fleeting, violent world that the Parkers could never escape.

And as the sun set on the quiet neighborhood, the house that had once been a home now felt like a tomb. There was no escape from what they had allowed into their lives. There was no turning back from the consequences of the shared economy.

And, as they stood in the dimly lit living room, their hearts pounding, they realized with chilling certainty that they would never be the same again.

"The Watcher's Journal"

Sarah and Tom had been living in their quiet suburban home for years, a place they had made their own. The small guest bedroom upstairs had always been empty, save for the occasional visitor or relative who needed a place to stay. But recently, with finances tighter than usual, they decided to rent out the space. The decision seemed simple enough. They listed the room online, and it didn't take long before they found someone—a man named Richard who was traveling for work. He was polite, courteous, and quickly agreed to the terms. He had no baggage, no strange requests. Just a simple need for a temporary place to stay.

Richard moved in, and life went on as usual. At first, everything seemed perfect. He was quiet, kept to himself, and Sarah and Tom barely saw him during the day. He was always out for work or meetings, and when he was home, he kept to his room. The house felt calm, peaceful, and they assumed the arrangement would be an easy one.

But then, after a few weeks, strange things started to happen.

Tom was the first to notice. One evening, while putting away some old books in the study, he stumbled upon a small notebook tucked behind a shelf. It was leather-bound, aged, and worn, with no markings on the cover. He assumed it was an old journal of Sarah's, or perhaps a forgotten piece from a past tenant, and left it on the table. When Sarah came in to take a look, she frowned, confused.

"This isn't mine," she said, flipping through it. The pages were filled with neat, precise handwriting, but the content was... unsettling. The first few pages were harmless enough, just observations about the weather, the neighborhood, but as Sarah read on, she began to feel a creeping unease.

The entries grew more specific, more personal.

"Sarah cooked pasta for dinner tonight. She hummed while chopping the onions. Tom came in and kissed her cheek before sitting down at the table. They're both wearing matching gray sweaters."

It was as if the journal's writer had been watching them—*stalking* them in their own home. Sarah's skin prickled as she turned the page, her heart beginning to race.

"Their dog is sleeping on the couch. Tom's glasses are on the coffee table. Sarah hasn't noticed me watching her through the window as she waters the plants."

The chill that crawled down her spine was unmistakable. The details were too precise, too personal. How could anyone know these things unless they were... *there*?

"What is this?" Sarah whispered, her voice shaking.

Tom's face had gone pale. "I don't know. This isn't okay. We need to talk to Richard."

They confronted Richard the next day. He was apologetic, even shocked by their discovery. "I... I didn't know how to stop. I just..." His voice trailed off as he tried to explain himself. "It's a habit. I've been doing it for years, keeping track of things, writing them down. It helps me focus. I didn't mean any harm. I didn't think you'd find it."

But as Sarah and Tom stood there, listening to his half-hearted explanations, something inside them snapped. This wasn't just a habit. This was something darker. Richard wasn't just observing them—he was cataloging every moment of their lives. The room suddenly felt smaller, tighter, as if the walls were closing in. They couldn't trust him anymore. He'd been *watching* them. And the more they thought about it, the more every small, odd moment began to feel sinister—the times they'd found their things moved slightly, the times Sarah would think she'd caught a glimpse of Richard's shadow at the corner of her eye.

Sarah took the journal and flipped to the last page. The entries were dated only a day before, and the words sent a cold wave of terror crashing over her:

"Sarah and Tom are talking to me now. I wonder if they know I've been here the whole time. I wonder how long they'll stay unaware of how much I've seen. It's too late for them to leave. They're already mine."

Her hands trembled as she closed the journal. She looked up at Tom, who was staring at her with wide eyes, his face pale, lips trembling. They both knew this wasn't just an innocent mistake. Richard wasn't just a quiet guest. He was a predator, and they had been the prey, unknowingly letting him into their lives.

They told him to leave, to pack his things and go, but Richard refused. He remained calm, almost unnervingly so, his smile never wavering. "I've never been this close to such a perfect couple," he said, his voice soft but deliberate. "You'll understand soon. I promise."

The door slammed behind him as he left, but the atmosphere in the house remained suffocating, like an invisible force still pressed against the walls. The house didn't feel like home anymore. It felt like a stage. They felt like actors trapped in someone else's twisted play.

For the next few days, they tried to resume normal life, but the dread only grew. They felt watched at every turn—by Richard's words, his eyes, his presence. The walls of the apartment seemed to echo with the traces of his gaze. The items in the house felt wrong—moved, shifted, placed in new spots where they didn't belong. The subtle details—the way their mugs were placed just slightly out of order, the way their bedroom door was ajar when they were sure they'd closed it—were enough to make their hearts race every time they entered a room.

Then, the noises began.

It started quietly at first—footsteps in the hall when they were alone, a whisper when the wind didn't blow. But the noises grew louder, more intrusive. It was as if Richard's presence was imprinted on the apartment, an echo of his obsession with them. The whispering turned into soft knocking, light tapping on the walls, a constant reminder that he was still there, even though he was gone.

One night, Sarah woke up to the feeling of being suffocated. She opened her eyes to see a shadowy figure standing at the foot of the bed. Her breath caught in her throat as she sat up, heart pounding, eyes straining in the darkness.

It was Richard's face. Not fully there, but his silhouette was unmistakable, watching them in the quiet, suffocating darkness. The face grinned, a twisted, knowing smile. "I'm still here," it whispered, just loud enough to hear.

Sarah screamed, waking Tom, but when they turned on the lights, the figure was gone. The room was empty, save for their own heavy breathing.

The terror didn't stop there. It escalated, night after night, until they couldn't tell if they were awake or asleep. Every shadow felt like Richard's eyes upon them. Every sound became a reminder that they were trapped—trapped in their own home, trapped by the consequences of their trust.

The walls closed in, and Sarah and Tom couldn't escape. Richard had already embedded himself too deeply in their lives, and the truth was undeniable: They had let the monster in. The apartment, once a peaceful retreat, had become a claustrophobic prison of paranoia, a place where the invisible presence of someone watching them never relented.

And now, every corner of the house was tainted by his obsession.

There was no escape.

"The Guest"

Mara was never the type to turn someone away. She lived alone in a modest one-bedroom apartment on the outskirts of the city, and while she enjoyed the solitude, there were times when loneliness would creep in like an unwelcome visitor. So, when she saw the ad—an international traveler in need of a place to stay for a few days—Mara didn't hesitate. The extra income would help pay for the rent, and it was just a couch, after all. Nothing too personal. She hadn't had a guest in a while, and the idea of sharing her space for a short time didn't seem so bad.

When Noah arrived, he was the epitome of charm. Tall, with an easy smile and a calming presence, he immediately made Mara feel at ease. He was soft-spoken, polite, and genuinely grateful for her hospitality. His stories about his travels, the places he had seen, and the people he had met made her feel as if she were part of something larger, as though her life—her quiet little apartment—wasn't just a dot on the map.

The first few days were easy. Noah was quiet, always reading or on his phone, never intruding. He'd make dinner sometimes, offering her a plate of whatever exotic dish he had concocted from ingredients she didn't recognize. He was kind, thoughtful even, and it was hard not to like him. But little by little, something about his presence started to shift.

It started with small gestures. One evening, Mara came home from work to find the apartment tidied up, her kitchen sparkling as if he had somehow anticipated her need for order. She smiled at the gesture, not thinking much of it. But then, over the following days, Noah began offering unsolicited advice on things he thought could be improved—how she should organize her closet, how she should arrange the furniture to better "flow" with the energy of the space. At first, it seemed like harmless suggestions. But they began to feel more like commands.

"You know, Mara," he said one evening, his voice smooth and gentle as he sat next to her on the couch, "if you moved that bookshelf across from the window, the light would be better. It would make the space feel more open."

Mara was taken aback by how certain he was, but the suggestion felt good, and she found herself agreeing. It was so simple, so small. Maybe it *would* make the space feel better, she thought.

As the days passed, Noah became more involved in her routine. He started accompanying her to the grocery store, walking beside her like a shadow. She felt strangely comforted by his presence—until the way he lingered over her shoulder, offering opinions on what she should buy, started to make her feel suffocated. Still, she pushed the feeling aside. After all, he had nowhere else to go, and he was just being friendly.

But the line between kindness and control began to blur.

One day, Mara came home early from work to find Noah sitting on the couch, staring at her phone. His expression was unreadable, his brow furrowed as he quickly put it down when she entered.

"You were looking at my phone?" she asked, feeling a cold pit settle in her stomach.

Noah smiled reassuringly, but it didn't reach his eyes. "I just wanted to see if you'd gotten the message from your friend Sarah. She's been trying to reach you."

Her heart skipped a beat. Sarah hadn't called, and Mara hadn't been expecting a message from her. "I—I can check it myself," she said, her voice tight.

But Noah didn't seem to hear her. Instead, he leaned in closer, his voice lower now, almost coaxing. "You trust me, don't you, Mara? I just want to make sure you're not missing anything. I only look out for you."

The way he said it made her skin crawl. There was an edge to his words, something sharp, something possessive.

"Of course I trust you," she said, trying to smile. But his eyes remained fixed on hers, piercing and unwavering, as though he were studying her every reaction.

Over the next few weeks, Noah's behavior became more erratic. He started showing up at her workplace during lunch breaks, waiting outside for her, even though she hadn't asked him to. His presence, once a comfort, now felt like an intrusion, like a shadow she couldn't shake. The messages, too—he started sending her texts every few hours, sometimes just a simple "How are you?" and other times something more unnerving, like "Don't forget your keys. I'll make sure you're safe."

One night, Mara came home to find the door slightly ajar. She didn't remember leaving it that way. Her pulse quickened as she stepped inside, the silence of the apartment wrapping around her like a thick fog. Then she saw him—Noah, standing in the hallway, a small smile playing on his lips.

"I noticed you left the door open," he said, almost too casually. "I wanted to make sure you were safe."

Her heart pounded. "I... I didn't leave it open," she said, her voice shaky. "Why were you standing there?"

"I just wanted to check in on you," he replied, his eyes locked onto hers, and for a moment, she thought she saw something dark flicker behind them. "You've been working hard. You deserve someone who watches over you."

Mara felt her skin prickle, a cold wave of fear washing over her. She wanted to leave, to scream, to tell him to leave her alone—but she didn't. Not yet.

Over the following days, the atmosphere in the apartment grew increasingly suffocating. She felt his presence everywhere—watching from the corners, waiting for her when she came back from errands. His questions became more intimate, more invasive. "Do you ever feel like you're just *going through the motions*? That you're living someone else's life?"

Mara found herself answering him, her words slipping out as if guided by some unseen force. His influence was subtle, but it was there—like an unseen hand tugging at the strings of her mind. The more he talked, the more she began to doubt herself, to question her own decisions. Could he be right? Could she trust herself?

One evening, after a particularly unsettling conversation, Mara found a note on the kitchen counter, scrawled in Noah's neat handwriting: "You *need* me, Mara. You'll see. You can't live without me."

Her blood ran cold. It wasn't just a suggestion anymore. It was a command.

Suddenly, everything in the apartment seemed to close in on her. The walls felt too close, the air too thick. She couldn't breathe, couldn't think. She needed to leave, to run away from him, but his words—those words—kept echoing in her mind. He was right. She couldn't live without him.

And that's when it hit her—the full, horrifying realization: she wasn't the one in control anymore. She hadn't been for a while.

The power he had over her, the way he had slowly twisted her thoughts, manipulating her with every word, every touch—it was all part of the game. And she had become the pawn.

The feeling of being trapped, of losing herself, consumed her. The apartment, once a place of safety, had become a prison. Noah's presence loomed over her like a shadow, a constant reminder that escape was impossible.

Mara looked at the door, at the world outside, but she didn't move.

And Noah, watching from the corner of the room, smiled. "I knew you'd come around."

"The Tenants"

The Lawson family had always considered themselves welcoming and open-minded. When their youngest child, Emma, went off to college, they decided to rent out the small downstairs apartment. The extra income would help with bills, especially after Tom's recent job loss. They thought it would be a simple arrangement, one where they could maintain their privacy while giving someone a quiet place to live.

They didn't expect much from the tenants—just someone who would respect the space and come and go without making waves. When Jacob and Heather arrived, they seemed like the perfect fit. Jacob was a writer, and Heather, his girlfriend, was a student. They were quiet, polite, and clean. They paid their rent on time, and at first, everything seemed ideal. They kept to themselves, barely crossing paths with the Lawsons.

But it wasn't long before small things started to feel... off.

At first, the family didn't notice it—just a sense that the house seemed quieter, the rooms colder when they came home. The bathroom door would be open when they were sure it had been closed. Little things were missing—Tom's spare change from his desk, a paperclip from the kitchen drawer—but they attributed it to forgetfulness or the occasional slip of memory. Maybe they were just imagining things.

But then, it became undeniable.

One evening, Sarah, the mother, came home from work early and found Jacob sitting in the living room, the TV muted. He didn't look at her as she entered. His eyes were fixed on a notebook, his pen scribbling furiously. At first, she didn't think much of it—he was probably working on his writing, as he often claimed. But when she caught a glimpse of the notebook, her stomach dropped.

The pages were filled with notes, not about his work—*her* work. About *her*. About the way she arranged the flowers on the coffee table, about the time she had yelled at Emma to clean her room, about the way she laughed after a joke at dinner. The notebook was filled with *her life*—intimate details, things only someone close to her would notice.

"Jacob," she asked, her voice trembling, "what is this? Why are you writing about me?"

His eyes didn't leave the page. "I'm just observing, Sarah," he said, his voice too calm, too casual. "It's for a project. I thought it might help me understand people better."

The hairs on the back of Sarah's neck stood up. The words didn't feel like an answer. They felt like a warning.

From that moment, it all started to unravel.

A week later, Sarah found a note slipped under the front door. It was a simple piece of paper, folded in half. It read: *I saw what you did last night.*

Her blood ran cold. There was no explanation. Just that cryptic line. She couldn't remember doing anything unusual. But the thought of being watched—*watched*—shook her to her core.

The dread deepened. Tom started to feel the pressure, too. The house, once a place of comfort, now felt like a cage. He would find his emails subtly altered, his work schedule somehow shifted when he hadn't made the changes. The family's private conversations were suddenly being interrupted by knocks on the door, sometimes in the middle of the night. Jacob and Heather seemed to know things they shouldn't. They would ask about Tom's job, about Sarah's past, as if they'd been digging into their private lives.

Then came the first confrontation.

Tom found Heather sitting in the kitchen late one night. She didn't acknowledge him at first, her eyes fixed on her phone screen. She was scrolling through something—something with his name on it. Something that made her smile, a smile that didn't reach her eyes.

"Hey," Tom said, his voice tight, "what are you doing?"

Heather's gaze slowly shifted to him. There was something dark in her expression. "Oh, nothing," she replied sweetly. "Just making sure I have all the facts. You wouldn't want me to share some of those, would you?"

Tom felt a chill wash over him. "What are you talking about?"

Heather's smile widened. "Well, it's funny. I found out a lot about you, Tom. All the things you thought were hidden. All those little secrets you thought no one would notice. It's amazing what a few minutes of looking can do."

Fear froze Tom in place. "You're crossing a line," he said, his voice wavering.

Heather stood up slowly, locking eyes with him. "Are you sure? Because I've already started sharing what I know with some people who are... interested in you. Interested in what you've been doing. It's only a matter of time before I share more. Unless, of course, you want to play along."

Tom's throat tightened. His mind raced, but he couldn't find the words. She had threatened him. She had *watched* him. It was no longer just about weird observations—it was about control.

The next morning, the tension was unbearable. Jacob and Heather's behavior grew more erratic. Jacob would sometimes appear in the middle of the day, standing silently in the hallway, staring at Sarah as she went about her business, never speaking, just watching. When she tried to confront him, he would laugh it off, claiming he was just "thinking."

Sarah and Tom tried to ignore the mounting dread. They tried to pretend they could live with it, but the weight of their unease was unbearable. They began to notice things—things they couldn't explain. Tom's car keys would disappear, only to reappear on the kitchen counter, not where he had left them. Their bank accounts were subtly altered, small amounts withdrawn for things they hadn't purchased. Every time they thought they had a moment of peace, something else would break their fragile sense of security.

Then came the final blow.

One evening, after a particularly tense confrontation, Sarah found a folder on the kitchen table, neatly placed there as if it had always belonged. Inside were photographs—photographs of her and Tom. The moments they'd thought were private, when they thought they were alone, were all captured in clear detail. Photos of Tom's late-night work calls, of Sarah standing at the window, of their daughter Emma walking to school. All taken without their knowledge. All watched, studied, and documented.

The last page of the folder was a printed letter, with a chilling message: *We're always watching. It's too late for you now.*

The walls of their home felt like they were closing in. The air grew thick with panic, with a sense of overwhelming dread. Every decision they had made—every action they had taken—had led them to this moment: a slow, insidious spiral into a nightmare they couldn't escape. Their privacy had been ripped away, and in its place was something far worse than they could have ever imagined. They were trapped in their own home, caught in the web of manipulation, blackmail, and control.

In the end, the Lawsons realized something even more terrifying: *the consequences of the shared economy weren't just financial.* It was a door they had opened to a nightmare. A nightmare where their lives were no longer their own. They had allowed strangers to watch them, to manipulate them, and now, there was no way out. The house that had once been their refuge had become their prison, and they were trapped within the walls they had once called home.

"The Water's Edge"

It seemed like a harmless idea at first—a simple way to make some extra cash. The summer heat was unbearable, and Sarah's pool was going unused, save for the occasional dip by her and her husband, Mark. The house was spacious, with a large, inviting pool in the backyard, perfect for anyone wanting to cool off. So, when Sarah listed the pool on a local rental app, she didn't expect much—just a few guests now and then. It was a popular service in their area; people came, swam, and left, paying a small fee for the privilege.

The first few guests were friendly, nothing unusual. They would arrive in groups, laughter filling the air, children running around the yard, playing. Sarah was happy with the arrangement. It brought in extra money, and the guests never overstayed their welcome. There was a peace to it. But as the weeks passed, Sarah began to notice a man who had been booking the pool more frequently than others. His name was Daniel. He always came alone. He was quiet, reserved, and polite, though something about him felt... off.

His presence was a shadow that seemed to linger long after he'd left. He always stayed until the pool was empty, after everyone else had left, spending hours in the water alone. Sarah didn't mind at first. He paid upfront, and that was all that mattered. But then, she started to notice the strange way he watched the pool, as though he was observing the water for something beyond the surface. He would occasionally take pictures with his phone, framing shots with an eerie precision, his eyes never leaving the lens.

One day, Sarah came outside to check on things, to find the pool area disturbingly quiet. The gate was unlocked, and there were no signs of anyone. Her heart skipped a beat when she noticed the pool cover was drawn across the water, a stark, heavy sheet that seemed out of place.

When she lifted the cover, her breath caught in her throat. The water was still, silent, unnervingly calm, but the surface was stained—dark red streaks curling at the edges of the pool. Blood. A chill ran through her as she looked at the pool deck. There were remnants of something—clothes, a towel with a handprint smeared in it, and, as her eyes moved to the far corner of the yard, a camera bag lying half open on the grass.

Her hand trembled as she reached down to examine it. Inside, she found a photo album. It wasn't just filled with pictures of the pool, of people laughing or swimming—it was something far darker. The first few images were of guests from the previous weeks, but as she flipped through the pages, her stomach twisted. The pictures turned from playful and carefree to something sinister. There were images of a woman's lifeless body, floating face down in the pool. Another photo showed a man with wide, glassy eyes staring blankly at the camera, his body held up by the water's edge.

Her pulse raced. These were no longer simple photos—they were gruesome stages of a killing. The images were framed deliberately, the bodies arranged as though posed for a photograph, the pool becoming a backdrop for something far darker than a swim.

A cold realization gripped Sarah—she was renting her pool to someone who was using it to stage something far more horrifying than innocent poolside fun. She had been unwittingly hosting the murder of people, turning her backyard into a macabre photo studio.

But there was no time to think further. Before she could process what was happening, a sound made her freeze—a door creaked open behind her. She spun around, her heart thudding in her chest. There, standing in the doorway of her house, was Daniel. His face was expressionless, like a predator who had been stalking its prey. His eyes narrowed as he took in the sight of Sarah holding the photo album, his lips curling into a faint, unsettling smile.

"I see you've found my work," he said softly, his voice almost a whisper, too calm for the situation.

Her hands shook. "What have you done? What is this?" Her voice cracked, a mix of anger and fear. "You've been killing people... right here... using my pool..."

Daniel didn't flinch. He stepped forward, his movements slow, deliberate. "I didn't kill anyone," he said, his tone like a lecture. "I just... captured something. People are fragile, Sarah. They're perfect for my art. They come here, they trust me, they enjoy the moment, and I capture it. The water makes them beautiful, makes them... still. There's something pure about that, don't you think?"

The air felt thick with dread, a suffocating presence filling the space between them. The tension was unbearable, the space shrinking as he closed the gap between them. "You can't undo what's been done," he continued, stepping closer. "It's already out there. You let me in. You shared your space. And now, you're part of it, too."

His words were like a death sentence. Sarah's mind raced, her body screaming for escape, but her legs wouldn't move. She wanted to shout, to run, to fight, but it was as if the air had been stolen from her lungs.

The sharp smell of chlorine mixed with something else—something more metallic—hung in the air, and the pool seemed to *wait* for her to react. She could almost hear the stillness of the water, the deep, unspoken presence of the horrors that had been staged there.

Suddenly, Sarah felt a cold hand on her shoulder. She whirled around, only to see Daniel's face inches from hers, his smile wide and manic. "The photos are already in the right hands. It's too late, Sarah. You're involved now. You can't escape."

Her body felt heavy, as though the weight of the pool, the weight of his words, was sinking into her very soul. The claustrophobia of the moment, the undeniable realization that her life had been invaded, took hold of her. She had been so naive—renting out her pool to a stranger. Now, it was too late to undo the damage.

Sarah's vision blurred as the ground seemed to tilt beneath her. She had opened the door to something she could never close. The consequences of sharing her space with someone so malevolent were now irreversible.

And as she looked back toward the pool, she realized with horror that she was no longer just a bystander. She had become part of the chilling art, trapped in the image he had captured, trapped in a nightmare she could never escape.

"The Tenants"

Mia was excited about her new apartment. The rent was cheap for the area, and the place was well-located, close to her new job and within walking distance of her favorite cafes. The shared space arrangement made sense. She'd be renting a room in an apartment with three others—people who, at least on paper, seemed like the perfect fit. They were professional, friendly, and even shared the same interests, which Mia thought was a good omen.

The first few days went smoothly. Her roommates—Nina, Max, and Stefan—seemed like normal people, if a bit eccentric. They were quiet, private, but kind enough when they interacted. Nina, a tall woman with pale skin and dark hair, had a soft smile that was welcoming, though there was always a hint of something off in her gaze. Max, quiet and lean, spent most of his time in his room, only emerging briefly to heat up food. Stefan, a muscular man with sharp features, was friendly but distant, always too busy to engage in much conversation. They didn't seem like a family, but they seemed fine.

But something about the apartment itself started to unsettle Mia. The walls were thin, and at night, the sounds from the other rooms were distorted. There were no loud conversations, no fights, but sometimes there were strange noises—whispers in the dark, shuffling footsteps in the hall when no one was around. The air in the apartment always felt too still, too thick, as if the oxygen itself was heavy with something that couldn't quite be named.

Then, one night, Mia woke up to the sound of footsteps in the hall. She glanced at her phone—2:47 AM. The others had been asleep when she'd gone to bed, and the sound didn't seem normal. The footfalls were slow, deliberate, dragging almost, as if someone was moving but didn't quite have the energy to walk properly. Mia pulled her blankets tighter around her and held her breath, hoping the sound would go away.

But it didn't.

Instead, it stopped at her door. Mia felt her heart leap in her chest. Her pulse quickened as the door handle slowly turned, just enough to make the faintest click, the kind that would be almost imperceptible to anyone else. The door creaked open, but Mia didn't move. She didn't dare make a sound. In the dim light from the hallway, she saw the shadow of someone standing in the doorway, but there was no one there when she peeked around the corner. The space was empty.

She was sure she had heard footsteps.

When she asked Nina the next morning, the woman smiled softly and brushed it off, claiming it was probably just a strange noise from the building, an old house settling. But Mia didn't feel reassured.

The strangest part was, the longer Mia stayed, the more she noticed her roommates' odd behaviors. They never seemed to eat normal food—just strange, unidentifiable dishes that they ate alone in their rooms. They were always awake late at night, and when Mia tried to join them for a late snack, they would quickly excuse themselves, disappearing into the shadows before she could ask more questions.

Nina, in particular, had a chilling habit. Whenever Mia was around, the woman would always look at her a bit too long, her eyes narrowing as if studying her. Sometimes, Mia caught her staring from across the room, her gaze unblinking, cold. Mia would smile politely, but Nina's expression never changed, never warmed.

One night, after hearing the strange footsteps again, Mia decided to confront Stefan, who had been sitting alone in the living room. He didn't turn to face her when she spoke, his back to her as he stared at the darkened television.

"Stefan, I keep hearing strange noises at night. It's—" Mia began, but her voice trailed off as she realized Stefan wasn't even blinking.

"Don't worry about it, Mia," his voice was raspy, low, and unnervingly calm. "You're imagining things. Go back to your room."

Mia felt a strange unease settle deep in her stomach. She had never heard him speak like that before, as though his voice wasn't entirely his own. The silence between them stretched, and she could feel her own heartbeat pounding in her ears. Stefan didn't move. He just sat there, staring ahead, not reacting at all.

The next day, Mia went to check her phone in the kitchen and found a strange message from an unknown number: *We see you, Mia. You belong to us.*

Her stomach churned. She had no idea how the message had arrived, but it felt all too real. Every part of her told her to leave, to run, but the apartment had become a cage. The walls were too close, and there was no way out. She asked Nina and Max about the message, but they played it off, offering her fake smiles, too eager to assure her that it was a mistake, a prank from someone who had access to her number.

But Mia knew. They were lying.

That night, as Mia lay in bed, trying to sleep despite the oppressive atmosphere, she heard the sounds again. This time, they were louder—closer. Someone was walking down the hallway, their feet dragging, slowly, agonizingly slowly. Mia's heart hammered in her chest. She dared not move, dared not make a sound.

The footsteps stopped at her door. There was a long pause, then the softest knock—a slow, deliberate rap, as if the person wanted her to know they were there, but didn't want to wake her.

She held her breath, too terrified to respond, her skin crawling. The door handle turned, but Mia didn't move. She couldn't. Then, the door creaked open.

Her room felt colder. Colder than it should have been. Her vision blurred, and she saw Nina standing in the doorway, staring at her with eyes that were black—completely black, like endless pits of shadow. The woman's lips curled into a twisted smile, her face stretching unnaturally wide. "You shouldn't have stayed, Mia," Nina whispered, her voice echoing with an eerie reverberation.

And then, before Mia could react, Nina stepped forward, but there was no warmth, no feeling of flesh. It felt like the darkness itself had taken form.

Mia screamed, but it was too late. As she tried to run, she felt the weight of the room close in, the walls pressing in around her like a vice. It wasn't just Nina. It was the whole apartment. The entire building seemed alive, breathing with malice, with intent. Stefan's and Max's faces—*blank*, hollow—appeared at the doorway. They weren't human. None of them were.

They were something else. Something ancient and hungry.

The darkness crept into her mind, her thoughts swirling as she realized she was trapped. No one had been human. No one had ever been real. They had just been waiting for her—waiting to claim her as their own.

And with that chilling realization, Mia was swallowed by the dark.

"The Hidden Poison"

Laura and Peter had always been a loving couple, close-knit and content in their quiet suburban home. Their lives were simple, yet fulfilling, until Peter lost his job at the start of the year. The financial strain was becoming unbearable, and the prospect of losing their home loomed like an ever-present shadow. One night, over a glass of wine, they made the decision to rent out part of their house—an unused guest bedroom—to help make ends meet.

They didn't expect much from the arrangement, just a tenant who could pay rent and stay out of the way. But when Thomas arrived, he seemed perfect. He was polite, well-spoken, and charming. He had a steady job in the city and seemed to need only a temporary place to stay while he worked on a project. He was clean, respectful, and never caused any trouble. Laura and Peter, relieved by the extra income, welcomed him into their home, grateful for the lifeline he seemed to offer.

At first, everything went smoothly. Thomas kept to himself, only occasionally engaging in small talk with Laura and Peter, always polite, always pleasant. He wasn't intrusive, rarely stayed in the common areas, and respected their privacy. The couple quickly grew accustomed to his presence—his quiet routine became part of the rhythm of their home.

But it didn't take long before things began to feel... off.

It started subtly. Peter and Laura both began to feel unusually tired. At first, it was just a little fatigue, a slight lack of energy they attributed to the stress of their changing circumstances. But then it worsened. Laura found herself waking up in the morning feeling like she hadn't slept at all. Her limbs felt heavy, her head foggy. Peter, usually a picture of health, started experiencing headaches and dizziness. Their appetites began to dwindle, and they both started losing weight. But nothing alarming enough to make them question the source. After all, they were both under a lot of stress.

Yet as the days passed, something darker began to settle over the house. The air felt thick, almost suffocating, as if the house itself was closing in around them. It wasn't just the physical symptoms—they started to feel *watched*. Sometimes, when they would return home after errands, they'd find the house strangely colder, or the curtains drawn shut even when they'd left them open. The feeling that someone had been in their space, had touched their things, became too pervasive to ignore.

One evening, Peter stumbled upon something he hadn't expected to see. He had been feeling dizzy all day, his vision blurry, his thoughts slow, and he had gone into the kitchen to grab some water. As he passed Thomas's room, he saw the door slightly ajar. He hesitated but walked past anyway, only to stop in his tracks when he saw something strange. On the small desk in the corner of Thomas's room was a bottle—a small vial, clear but with a faintly green tint. It looked like a chemical, the kind of thing Peter had seen before, on old medicine bottles or laboratory supplies.

A sick feeling gnawed at his gut. He wanted to ignore it, to think he was imagining things, but his mind wouldn't let go of the thought. What was it? What was Thomas doing with it?

That night, the couple's health deteriorated even further. Laura woke up in the middle of the night, gasping for breath, her chest constricted as if an invisible hand was tightening around her lungs. Her skin was pale, damp with sweat. Peter, too, had trouble breathing, and his joints felt as if they were made of stone. Neither of them could remember a time they had felt so utterly drained, so incapable of moving or thinking. They staggered through their days, barely managing to function, while a dark, oppressive force seemed to weigh down the house.

It wasn't until Laura began to have vivid dreams that the terror truly set in. In her dreams, she would see Thomas standing in the kitchen late at night, pouring something into their water glasses, watching them drink. The liquid in the glass would shimmer, taking on a faint green hue before it disappeared into their bodies. She woke in a cold sweat, her heart racing, her throat tight.

The next morning, the dread became impossible to ignore. She tried to confront Thomas, but when she entered the kitchen, he was already there, drinking his coffee as if nothing had happened. He looked at her with that calm, unsettling smile, as if he had no idea why she seemed so off. But his eyes—those eyes—never left hers. They seemed to pierce through her, as if they were seeing straight into her soul.

The feeling of being watched became unbearable. They weren't just *being watched* anymore—they were being controlled. The physical symptoms only grew worse: nausea, severe fatigue, dizziness, vomiting. Laura began to suspect that the strange vial she had seen wasn't just for some harmless experiment—it was poisoning them, slowly, subtly, until they couldn't escape. And Thomas, with his quiet demeanor and calm words, was the orchestrator of their suffering. But why?

One evening, after she and Peter both fell asleep on the couch, they woke in the middle of the night to the sound of footsteps approaching them. The door to the living room creaked open, and they saw Thomas standing in the doorway, holding something in his hand. He didn't speak—he just watched them, his expression unreadable, his face too pale in the dim light.

Suddenly, the realization hit. They weren't just ill. They weren't just tired. They were *dying*. Thomas had been poisoning them—slowly, carefully, with whatever chemical was in that vial. The weight of it all crashed down on them. They were trapped in their own home, slowly suffocating in the grip of someone they had trusted.

"Why are you doing this?" Peter rasped, his voice weak from the strain of his body fighting the toxins that had been silently coursing through him for weeks.

Thomas smiled, his eyes cold and indifferent. "You weren't supposed to find out so soon," he said softly. "But it's already too late for you."

The words hung in the air like a death sentence.

The next few days blurred together. They tried to leave, to escape, but they could barely stand, let alone make it out the door. The world outside the house felt so distant, so unreachable. Every time they moved, the darkness seemed to follow them, as though the house itself was alive and suffocating them.

As the poison continued to work its way through their bodies, their sense of time became warped, their thoughts disjointed and muddled. They couldn't remember what day it was, or what had been real. The house, once a place of comfort, had turned into a prison, and Thomas—*the tenant*—had become their warden. His control over them had seeped into every corner of their lives, every breath they took.

And in the final moments of their minds fading, Sarah and Peter knew with chilling certainty: there was no escape. No one would believe them. No one could save them. They had trusted a stranger—someone who had quietly slipped into their lives and, piece by piece, had taken everything from them.

The last thing they saw was Thomas standing at the doorway, holding the vial. His cold smile was the last thing they saw before the darkness consumed them completely.

"The Artist's Work"

Kate and Paul had always taken pride in their home. It was a cozy, old house in a quiet neighborhood—a sanctuary they'd carefully curated over the years. The bright walls were adorned with art, the floors covered in warm rugs, and the air always smelled of freshly brewed coffee. Life had been good. But when Paul's job offered him an unexpected transfer across the country, the financial burden of maintaining the house on just Kate's income grew heavy. The thought of downsizing felt too painful. So, they decided to rent out the spare bedroom to a tenant. It wasn't supposed to be a permanent arrangement—just a way to make ends meet during their transition.

That's when they met Lucas, the artist.

Lucas seemed perfect for the space. A quiet, reserved man in his mid-thirties, he was a traveling artist with an air of mystery about him. He had a charming smile and an enthusiasm for the house that made Kate feel like it was the perfect fit. He promised he wouldn't disturb their routines, and after a brief conversation, they agreed to let him stay for a few months. He moved in quickly, and the first few days were uneventful—he spent most of his time in his room, painting, creating, or working on sketches. But soon, things began to shift.

It started with the odd noises at night. At first, Kate chalked it up to the house settling, the creaking of old wood beams, or the wind whipping through the trees outside. But as the days passed, the noises grew louder, more deliberate—scratching sounds in the walls, the muffled thud of something heavy being dropped, whispers in the corners of rooms where no one was present. They weren't just sounds of the house settling anymore; they were something *else*.

One evening, as Paul was working late, Kate decided to investigate. The house was eerily quiet, save for the unsettling sounds coming from down the hall—Lucas's room. She hesitated for a moment, but curiosity gnawed at her, and she crept toward the door.

She stood still outside his room, her breath shallow, as she heard what sounded like low chanting. It was rhythmic, almost hypnotic, but there was something unsettling in the cadence. It wasn't just a prayer or a song—it was a sound meant to *draw something in.*

She knocked once, quickly, but there was no response. Hesitantly, she opened the door, only to freeze in place. The room was dark, save for a single dim light hanging from the ceiling, casting elongated shadows across the walls. Lucas was standing in the middle of the room, his back to her, facing a large canvas. He wasn't painting. He was... *drawing something.* With dark charcoal, he scrawled symbols and runes along the walls, the floor covered in strange, unnatural patterns. There was something otherworldly about it, like the markings were alive, pulsating with a quiet energy.

Kate felt a chill creep up her spine, a cold knot tightening in her stomach. The air in the room was thick, suffocating, like something had invaded the space. It wasn't just the room—it felt as if the house itself was holding its breath.

"What are you doing?" Kate's voice trembled as she spoke, the words leaving her lips more weakly than she had intended.

Lucas turned slowly, a blank expression on his face. His eyes were wide, his pupils dilated, as if something had overtaken him. "I'm just... finishing my work," he said softly, his voice almost mechanical. "It's for the art. You wouldn't understand. It's part of the process."

Kate recoiled at the dark, hollow look in his eyes. Something in his gaze felt empty, as if he wasn't fully there, as if he was staring through her. The room was stifling now, the oppressive energy from the symbols seeping into her skin, as if the walls themselves were closing in. She turned quickly, closing the door behind her and retreating back to the living room, where she tried to shake the feeling of dread that had settled in her bones.

Over the following days, the house seemed to change. The once warm, welcoming walls now felt cold and oppressive. The strange noises continued, and Kate noticed more and more oddities—scratches on the floor, burnt candles scattered in corners, bits of torn paper with incomprehensible writing tucked into strange places. Lucas had begun to transform the house into his studio—a studio that felt more like a place of ritual than of art. Every surface seemed marked by some dark presence, every corner filled with the scent of something unfamiliar, something like incense and decay.

One evening, Paul came home early from work to find Kate standing in the kitchen, staring out the window with wide eyes.

"What's wrong?" he asked, noticing the unease in her expression.

"I don't know," Kate whispered, her voice strained. "It's like something's wrong with this house. It's *him*—he's doing something in there. He's not just painting, Paul. I think he's... *performing rituals.*"

Paul laughed nervously at first, but when he saw the genuine fear in her eyes, he stopped. He hadn't noticed the strange things Kate was talking about, but her fear was real. He'd also noticed the oppressive air in the house—the subtle unease that never seemed to go away.

Later that night, they confronted Lucas together. He was in his room, the door open just slightly, the faint glow of a candle flickering from inside. As they entered, they saw something truly horrifying.

The floor was covered in an intricate web of symbols, each one glowing faintly in the dim light. A small, black book lay open on the floor, its pages filled with pages of runes and diagrams. On the wall, another series of marks had been painted in blood, redder than anything they'd seen before, twisted in ways that made no sense.

"I told you, it's for the art," Lucas said, his voice detached, as if he was saying it for the hundredth time. His eyes were wide, manic, his body stiff as if he were under some sort of trance. "You don't understand. It's all a part of it. The art takes something... something more. It demands sacrifice."

A cold chill filled the room, and Kate felt her knees give way beneath her. Paul stepped forward, his voice rising in panic. "What are you talking about, Lucas? This isn't *art*. You're doing something else here. This is *wrong*."

But Lucas didn't respond. Instead, he stepped backward into the shadows, a low laugh escaping from his throat—a laugh that sounded hollow and dark, filled with something far more sinister than mere amusement.

The room began to spin, the walls seeming to close in around them. The symbols on the floor seemed to pulse with energy, the air thick with a heavy, unnatural silence. Kate's breath quickened, her pulse hammering in her ears, as the realization sank in—Lucas wasn't just an artist. He had opened a door, a door to something ancient, something dark, something they couldn't control.

Suddenly, the house felt like a tomb, and they were trapped within it. The door to the living room slammed shut, and the light flickered, plunging the room into darkness. They could hear his steps now, moving silently in the shadows, his whispers growing louder, filled with malicious intent.

Kate and Paul tried to run, but the house wouldn't let them go. The doors wouldn't open. The walls closed in, and the darkness seemed to take on a life of its own, suffocating them, pulling them deeper into the nightmare Lucas had crafted.

As they realized with horror that they could never escape, the last thing they heard was Lucas's voice, a faint whisper in the dark: "You'll be a part of it now, forever."

"The Silent Watcher"

Jenna had always been a trusting person. When her new job moved her to the city, she decided to rent out her spare bedroom to make ends meet. Her apartment was small but cozy, with warm light filtering through the large windows in the living room. It had always felt like a safe haven, a place where she could relax after a long day of work. The idea of sharing the space seemed harmless at first—just a way to offset her bills and meet new people.

When Ian reached out about the room, he seemed perfect. He was polite, well-spoken, and offered to pay several months' rent upfront. He mentioned he was a freelance photographer, someone who traveled often, and needed a quiet place to stay while he worked on a personal project. His profile was full of positive reviews, and when they met in person, he seemed kind enough.

Jenna didn't think much of it when Ian moved in. He was quiet, kept to himself, and didn't intrude on her routines. Most days, he would come and go at odd hours, never staying in the apartment for long. She felt secure in the thought that they were just two people coexisting in the same space, each with their own lives.

But the first sign that something wasn't right came when Jenna started noticing odd things. She would find her personal items moved slightly—her books out of place on the bookshelf, her keys on the kitchen counter when she swore she had left them in the hallway. She tried to ignore it, convincing herself it was just her mind playing tricks on her.

Then came the strange sounds. It started with what she thought was faint clicking noises late at night. At first, she dismissed it as the creaks of an old apartment building, but it happened so regularly—always at night—that it began to gnaw at her. There were whispers, too, when she was alone in the house, low murmurs that seemed to come from nowhere, just at the edge of her hearing.

One evening, Jenna came home to find the apartment unnervingly still. The lights in the living room were off, but as she entered her bedroom, she noticed something strange—her laptop was open on the desk. She hadn't left it on, and she distinctly remembered shutting it before leaving. Her heart skipped a beat as she approached the desk, and that's when she noticed it—there, just beneath the laptop's edge, was a small black device, almost hidden but too obvious to be a coincidence.

A camera.

She froze, her mind racing as panic slowly began to settle in. She immediately checked the apartment. The bathroom mirror, the living room shelf, even behind the picture frames—hidden cameras, small and discreet, tucked away in every corner of the apartment. The realization hit her like a punch to the stomach. Ian had been watching her—watching *everything*.

Her mind spun with the horrifying implications. Had he been recording her? Watching her when she changed, when she slept, when she was alone, thinking she was safe? She felt exposed, vulnerable in every inch of her own home.

Her breath caught in her throat as she began to search the rest of the apartment, her heart racing. Every room was the same—cameras hidden in plain sight, their lenses small and unassuming, yet insidious. They were in the kitchen, behind her couch, even in the hallway, tucked behind light fixtures. The house, once a safe refuge, had become a prison—a space she could no longer trust.

Jenna tried to confront Ian. Her voice trembled as she asked him about the cameras, her fingers shaking as she pointed to the devices hidden around the apartment. Ian's response was calm, too calm, as though he had anticipated this moment.

"I didn't mean to make you uncomfortable," Ian said, his voice smooth, almost soothing. "I was just... gathering material for my project. You know, I'm a photographer. These kinds of things—" He gestured to the cameras, "—they help me capture the truth, the real, unfiltered moments. It's not personal. I wasn't trying to invade your privacy. You're just... so interesting to watch."

Jenna recoiled at his words. "You can't just *watch* me like that!" she screamed. "This is my home! I trusted you!"

Ian smiled, that same calm smile. "I'm not doing anything wrong. You're not understanding. You see, you're part of my work now. You can't just leave it behind. You're a part of this. We're all part of this."

Her stomach twisted with the sick realization that he had planned this all along. The cameras weren't for some innocent project—they were part of a twisted, manipulative game. He had been studying her, gathering intimate details about her life, her routines, the way she moved, the way she existed in the space. He knew her better than she knew herself.

"I'm going to delete everything," Jenna said, her voice shaking with anger. "You're sick, Ian. You're sick, and you're going to leave. Now."

But Ian didn't react to the command. Instead, his eyes darkened, and his smile never faltered. "No, you don't get it. You can't delete it. You can't delete what's already been captured. What's already been seen. It's too late for that."

A cold sweat broke out on Jenna's skin as he stepped closer, his movements slow and deliberate. She backed away, her heart pounding in her chest. The walls of the apartment, which once felt like home, now felt like a cage. She wanted to escape, to run, but the door was closed. She was trapped, just like the moments he had so carefully documented.

"You're mine now," he whispered, his voice low and filled with something far more sinister than mere control. "I'll make sure everyone sees. Everyone knows."

The terror surged in her chest as she realized the full extent of his manipulation. Ian had crossed a line from mere voyeurism to something far more dangerous—blackmail. He could destroy her. He could expose her, twist her into something she wasn't, make her life fall apart with a simple press of a button.

The weight of the situation crashed down on her. Her mind raced, but her body felt numb. She had no way out. No one would believe her. Who would take her seriously? She had trusted him, invited him into her home, and now there was no escape from the consequences of that decision.

The room, the apartment, the walls, the cameras—all of them pressed in on her, trapping her in a nightmare. The air was thick with the knowledge that she was no longer in control of her life. Ian had her in his grasp, and she couldn't fight back.

She was no longer safe in her own home.

"The Watchers"

The Devereux family had always been kind and welcoming. When their children moved out, leaving them with an empty nest, they saw an opportunity to make some extra income by renting out the spare rooms in their large house to tourists. The money from the occasional visitor would help with bills, especially with Sarah's recent retirement and Carl's growing medical expenses. It was an easy decision—they'd done their research, checked all the references, and were confident the arrangement would be harmless.

Their first guests, a young couple named Jason and Melissa, arrived with smiles and promises of respectful, quiet stays. They were only supposed to be there for a weekend, and the Devereuxs barely even saw them—just a few exchanges in passing, polite hellos, and pleasantries. Everything seemed perfect, like an ideal arrangement. The couple left with a thank-you note and a small gift, and the Devereuxs felt good about helping people out.

But after they left, things started to feel... off.

It started small—odd noises at night. Carl, who had trouble sleeping due to his health, would sometimes hear footsteps in the hallway, followed by the sound of faint whispers. The sounds always came late, long after the family had gone to bed. Sarah dismissed it as the house settling or her husband's tired mind playing tricks on him. But Carl insisted something was wrong, that he heard strange things in the night—noises that shouldn't have been there.

Then came the stains. They weren't much at first, just small, dark spots that appeared near the doorframe of the guest bedroom, a few marks on the carpet. At first, Sarah just assumed someone had spilled something. But when she cleaned it, the stains came back, always in the same spots. It was like a persistent reminder that something wasn't quite right.

But the real horror didn't reveal itself until the next group of guests arrived.

The tourists, a quiet family of four, seemed pleasant enough at first. They had young children, a girl and a boy, both under the age of ten. Sarah and Carl greeted them warmly and showed them to their rooms, thinking it would be another uneventful stay. But as the days passed, Sarah began to notice something strange. The children would wander the house at odd hours, their footsteps too light for their size, their eyes too wide as if they were peering into something they shouldn't be seeing.

Sarah brushed it off—kids, she thought. They were probably just exploring. But then, one night, while Carl was out at a doctor's appointment, Sarah was in the kitchen, preparing dinner, when she caught a glimpse of something out of the corner of her eye. Through the window, she saw the husband and wife standing in the backyard, staring at her through the glass. Their expressions were unreadable—cold, emotionless, as if they were just watching her, waiting for something. She turned to face them, but when she looked back, they were gone, vanishing into the darkness like they had never been there at all.

She shook her head, trying to dismiss the growing sense of unease gnawing at her. But that night, the real horror began.

Carl returned home to find Sarah in a state of panic. She had gone into the guest room to make sure everything was in order, but when she opened the closet door, she found something that made her blood run cold. The walls of the closet were covered in photographs—hundreds of them, some of Sarah and Carl, others of their children when they were younger, some images of people they didn't recognize, and others... darker, more disturbing. There were photos of their family—captured without their knowledge, their faces contorted in fear, pain, and confusion. The couple's faces were in some of the shots, watching them from the shadows as if someone had been hiding, waiting, recording every moment.

Her breath hitched in her chest as she looked at the photos, the chilling realization sinking in. They had been *watched*—but who? Who had done this? How long had it been going on? She was shaking as she showed Carl the photos, and that's when he realized something even more terrifying.

The family of four had been staying in their guest room. The husband and wife, who seemed so friendly, had been the ones behind this, the ones behind the hidden cameras. But it wasn't just the photos—it was the *footage*. On a small SD card found in the closet, Sarah found hundreds of hours of video—footage of their home, of every room, every corner, including the most intimate moments. It was as if they had been watched the entire time, like their privacy had been sold away without them knowing.

But it wasn't just the family next door. The deeper they dug, the more horrifying the truth became. Sarah found links to an underground website—hidden behind layers of encryption and passwords—that posted *live streams* of families' homes. These streams were marketed as part of an *exclusive content* service. When she clicked on one of the videos, her stomach turned. It was a live stream of their own home, the camera angles perfectly positioned to capture every movement.

As they explored the site, they found other videos—others who had been invited to rent their homes, not knowing they were part of something far darker. The family of four were not tourists—they were operators, setting up the cameras, recording the footage, and selling it online as part of a black market snuff film ring.

Fear gripped Sarah and Carl's hearts as they realized the full extent of what was happening. They had been a part of something that went far beyond their comprehension. The house they thought was their safe space, their sanctuary, had become a stage for something unspeakable. They had been unwitting participants in a twisted, voyeuristic business.

As the dread settled in, they made a plan to confront the family. But when they returned to the guest room, it was empty. The family was gone—disappeared into the night, leaving behind only the remnants of their twisted game.

They thought they were safe. But the truth was worse than they could have imagined. The footage was already out there. It had already been shared, sold, and viewed by strangers. There was no escape. The cameras, the recordings, the dark network—it was too late to undo what had been done.

They were forever trapped, watched, and exploited, their privacy stripped away in an instant. And as Sarah looked at the empty guest room where the family had once stayed, she knew there was no escape from the consequences of their decision to rent out their home.

The house, once their safe haven, had become a prison.

"The Office Next Door"

Ryan had always been a professional. After years of working in the corporate world, he had finally made the leap into freelancing, setting up his own small office in a shared space in the heart of the city. It was an ideal arrangement—affordable, clean, and filled with like-minded individuals who came and went, working on everything from graphic design to consulting. It was the type of place that encouraged networking and collaboration, and Ryan enjoyed the quiet, communal atmosphere.

His office neighbor, a man named Chris, was new to the space. At first glance, he seemed unremarkable—a man in his thirties, always neatly dressed in a suit, with a kind smile and a calm, collected demeanor. He didn't say much at first, but after a week or two, Chris started to introduce himself to Ryan, and they struck up occasional conversations in the break room or by the coffee machine. Chris spoke in measured tones, never sharing too much about himself, always quick to deflect personal questions. It was odd, but Ryan didn't think much of it. Freelancers were often introverted, and besides, it wasn't like they were best friends—they shared an office, nothing more.

The strange things started when Ryan began to notice that Chris was always working late. Late into the night, long after the other tenants had left for the day, Chris would be at his desk, typing away on his computer. Ryan assumed it was just the demands of his business, though he couldn't help but feel an underlying sense of unease watching the man work alone, his face illuminated by the glow of the screen.

It wasn't until Ryan overheard a conversation one evening that the first warning bell rang. He had stayed late to finish up a project, and as he was walking back to his office, he heard Chris speaking on the phone in a low, urgent voice. He couldn't make out the words, but the tone was sharp, commanding. It sounded like a business call—but there was something cold in the way Chris spoke, as if the conversation was about more than just commerce. Ryan paused in the hallway, instinctively pressing his back against the wall, straining to listen. He heard Chris say, "Get it done by tomorrow, or we'll have a problem." There was a pause, then the sound of a click, followed by a tense silence.

Ryan quickly returned to his office, brushing off the strange feeling growing in his chest. Maybe it was just business stress. Maybe Chris was involved in something more intense, but it wasn't his concern. At least, not yet.

The next few days were filled with small, unsettling moments. Ryan began to notice packages being delivered to Chris's office—odd packages, usually wrapped in brown paper with no return address. At first, Ryan thought nothing of it. Perhaps Chris was getting supplies for a new project. But the frequency of the deliveries soon increased, as did the sense of unease Ryan felt every time he passed by Chris's office. The man seemed to be involved in something secretive—something Ryan couldn't quite put his finger on.

Then came the first sign of something truly wrong.

Ryan had been working late one evening, the office quiet except for the hum of his computer. He decided to take a break, stretching his legs and walking down the hallway to the bathroom. As he passed by Chris's office, the door was slightly ajar. Through the gap, Ryan saw Chris with another man—a stranger he didn't recognize—standing in front of a desk covered with stacks of cash. They were talking in low voices, too quietly for Ryan to hear the words. But when the man handed Chris a briefcase, something inside Ryan shifted. His stomach dropped.

The door was quickly closed, but the image of the exchange stuck with him. Something was happening in that office, something illegal. Ryan's mind raced as he tried to push the thought away, but the truth was slowly sinking in. Chris wasn't just running a legitimate business—he was involved in something darker.

Over the next few days, Ryan's unease grew into dread. He started noticing small things—shifts in Chris's behavior, the dark circles under his eyes, the strange people coming and going at all hours. And then, one afternoon, as he was working on a report, the office door swung open, and Chris entered, his face pale and drawn.

"We need to talk," Chris said, his voice low, his eyes darting around as if he feared someone might overhear.

Ryan hesitated, then nodded. "What's going on, Chris?"

"I'm in some trouble," Chris confessed, leaning against the door, his voice trembling. "It's... it's bigger than I expected. Things have gone wrong. I've made some enemies."

Ryan felt a chill run down his spine, but he couldn't look away. There was something in Chris's face, something raw, something desperate.

"What are you talking about?" Ryan asked.

Chris took a deep breath. "I'm involved in something I shouldn't be. I thought I could get out, but now I can't. It's too late. They won't let me go."

Ryan didn't understand what Chris meant at first, but then the man's next words made his blood run cold.

"They're coming for me, Ryan. But they won't just come for me—they'll come for everyone involved. And if you're close to me, you'll be dragged into it too."

Chris was shaking now, his eyes wild. "I'm not asking for your help. I'm just telling you to stay out of it. Don't get involved. It's too late for me, but you can still walk away."

Ryan's heart was pounding in his chest as he processed the words. The quiet, unassuming man he had shared an office with was involved in something much larger than either of them had anticipated—a criminal operation that, once exposed, could drag Ryan down with it.

He didn't know what to do. He wanted to walk away, to leave the office and never look back. But the truth was clear now: there was no escape. Chris was too deeply embedded in the operation, and by association, Ryan was already marked.

That evening, when Ryan returned home, he couldn't shake the feeling of being watched. Every noise, every shadow felt like a threat. His phone buzzed—a message from an unknown number: *We know what you've seen. It's too late to run.*

The next few days blurred into one long nightmare. Ryan tried to cut ties with Chris, but it was no use. Strangers started showing up at the office, the atmosphere thick with tension. The illegal operation was unraveling, and Chris's troubles were spilling over. Threats came in the form of veiled warnings, subtle at first, but increasingly violent. The people involved in the operation weren't just criminals—they were monsters, and now they were targeting Ryan.

And then, one evening, after returning to his office late, Ryan found the door ajar. Inside, his desk had been ransacked, his files torn apart. The walls were covered in strange symbols, hastily drawn, a sign of something dark and malicious. His heart pounded as he realized the full extent of the danger he was in.

He tried to escape. He tried to leave everything behind. But it was no use. The men who had been operating in the shadows had found him, and they weren't just taking Chris—they were coming for everyone who had been involved, everyone who knew too much.

Ryan's worst fear had come true: he had unknowingly walked into a world of crime and horror, a world that wouldn't let him go. The shared workspace, once a neutral ground, had become a prison—a place where trust had been shattered, and escape was impossible.

As the men entered the office, Ryan realized there was no running, no way out. The consequences of his actions—his innocent choice to rent space in a shared office—had led him to this terrifying end.

"The Guests"

For Clara and Mark, the decision to rent out the extra rooms in their house seemed like an innocent one. They had lived in their home for years, and the rising costs of living were beginning to take a toll. Their two children had moved out, and the large space felt empty, hauntingly quiet. When Clara came across an ad online about renting out spare rooms to long-term tenants, she thought it would help them stay afloat.

They didn't need much. Just a few extra months of rent to keep them comfortable. They didn't want anything more than quiet, responsible renters. When Ian arrived, he seemed like the perfect fit. In his mid-thirties, well-dressed and clean-cut, Ian was polite, well-spoken, and respectful of their space. He'd just landed a job in the city and needed somewhere quiet to settle in while he figured things out. Clara and Mark welcomed him into their home with open arms, confident in their decision.

For the first few weeks, everything went smoothly. Ian stayed to himself, coming and going quietly. He was respectful, never intrusive, and kept his room neat. But then, small things began to shift—subtle changes that set Clara on edge.

One morning, she found a strange smell in the house, a sharp, pungent scent that lingered in the air, even after she opened the windows. It wasn't the typical smell of food or cleaning supplies. It was something darker, something metallic and acrid. When she asked Ian about it, he assured her it was nothing—just some new spices he was experimenting with for a dish he was preparing. Clara didn't think much of it. Maybe it was just his new cooking experiment.

But then there were the people.

At first, it was just one man who came to visit Ian late at night. The man was tall, his face obscured by a hood, and his voice deep and unsettling. He came and went quietly, and Ian always made a point to introduce him to Clara and Mark as a "friend from work" when they encountered him in passing. The man never lingered long, always leaving by the time morning came. Still, the visits felt wrong, like something was being hidden behind closed doors.

Then came the other visitors—one after another, always different people, always arriving late in the evening, always leaving before sunrise. Some of them were scruffy, others well-dressed, but none of them ever seemed to stay long enough to get to know them. There was something off about them, an air of secrecy that hung around every interaction. Clara's gut twisted every time she noticed one of them lurking by the door, glancing over their shoulder, as if making sure no one was watching.

Clara tried to brush it off, telling herself that maybe they were just Ian's colleagues or friends from out of town, but the anxiety in her stomach grew with each new face. Mark, too, started to feel the strain. They had their suspicions but couldn't bring themselves to confront Ian. They didn't want to seem paranoid. But one night, after the man from before had come to visit again, Mark decided to follow him.

What he found made his blood run cold.

The man had gone straight to the back of the house, disappearing into the garage. Mark's breath caught in his throat as he moved silently toward the door, his heart hammering in his chest. Through a small crack in the door, he saw them—five or six men, standing around a table in the dim light. It wasn't just the odd visitors or the strange behavior—it was the way they spoke in low, urgent whispers, the way they passed around items on the table, each one wrapped in plastic, almost like... *drugs*. Mark couldn't see everything clearly, but the images were enough to send a chill through his bones.

The next morning, Mark confronted Ian. His voice was steady but full of hidden rage. "What the hell's going on, Ian? Who are these people? What are you doing in my house?"

Ian just smiled, his expression cold and unreadable. "Nothing to worry about, Mark. It's just business. I'll make sure they don't disturb you."

But his words didn't reassure Mark. They made his blood run cold. Something was happening, and it was getting worse.

That night, Clara and Mark were woken by a loud bang downstairs, followed by shouting. Clara's heart dropped into her stomach as she quickly got out of bed, rushing down the stairs to find Ian arguing with another man in the living room. The stranger was wild-eyed, his clothes torn, his voice hoarse as he yelled at Ian. Clara could barely make out the words, but she caught the phrases *"you said you'd help"* and *"this is your fault."*

Before she could ask what was going on, the man lunged at Ian, and a fight broke out. The sound of fists slamming against flesh echoed through the house, filling Clara with terror. Mark rushed downstairs, pulling the man off Ian, but the violence continued, each second dragging on like an eternity. By the time the struggle ended, the stranger was unconscious on the floor, blood staining the carpet.

Ian stood above him, breathing heavily, his face pale and tense. He didn't say a word. He just stared at Mark and Clara, as if daring them to speak.

"What the hell are you involved in?" Mark demanded, his voice shaking.

Ian looked at them, his eyes devoid of any remorse. "This was never your business. It was a mistake to let you into it."

The next few days felt like a dream—a nightmare that wouldn't end. The house, once a place of safety, had become a war zone. Clara and Mark tried to call the police, but Ian had warned them—he knew what they were doing, and if they tried to go to the authorities, they would regret it. Every move they made seemed to lead them deeper into the chaos. The men, the threats, the danger—all of it closed in around them.

One afternoon, while Clara was cleaning the kitchen, she noticed something strange outside the window—a black car parked across the street, its engine idling. As she watched, it became clear that the man sitting in the driver's seat was watching their house. And then, as if on cue, the doorbell rang. When Clara answered it, there was no one there—just a note, neatly folded and pressed against the door.

The note was simple, its message chilling: *We know everything. You'll never leave.*

As the days turned into weeks, Clara and Mark realized the full extent of their situation. The visitors were no longer just a nuisance—they were dangerous. They were part of something bigger, something far more sinister than either of them had imagined. Ian had led them into a criminal operation, and there was no escape. Every time they tried to fight back, the threats only became more menacing, more relentless. Their home was no longer a place of comfort. It had become a trap.

Finally, when they attempted to flee, they found their car vandalized, their phones hacked, and their lives slowly deteriorating under the weight of the consequences. Ian's business, his criminal empire, had left them broken, terrified, and trapped in a world they never asked for.

And as the walls closed in around them, Clara realized the terrifying truth: There was no escape from the consequences of the shared economy. The decisions they had made in search of a simple solution had led them straight into the heart of a nightmare, and now, there was no way out.

"The Ride"

The Martins had always been a family of simple pleasures. Their suburban home was modest but warm, filled with the scent of home-cooked meals and the soft laughter of their two children, Ethan and Lily. Mark and Sarah, both hardworking and kind-hearted, prided themselves on their strong family bond. Their lives were quiet, comfortable—nothing ever out of the ordinary.

When Sarah saw the ad online, it seemed like a harmless opportunity. Their car, a reliable but aging sedan, sat unused most of the time, especially with Sarah working from home and Mark commuting by train. So, when the opportunity to share it with a stranger came up—through one of those "shared economy" apps—she thought, why not? It would be a good way to offset the cost of the car's upkeep.

Enter Daniel. He was a quiet man, perhaps in his mid-thirties, polite and well-spoken. He had just moved to the area and needed a car for short trips while he settled into his new job. He didn't seem like the kind of person to cause any trouble. He was polite, punctual, and respectful. Sarah was immediately comfortable with him. She even found him reassuring when he mentioned that he had recently come from a small town and was looking for a fresh start.

For the first few weeks, everything was fine. Daniel would occasionally pick up the car for a few hours and return it in the same condition. Sarah had no complaints. She would even leave a note on the seat to remind him of some minor details about the car—like the seat settings or where the spare tire was stored—but other than that, there was little communication.

That was, until the night Sarah received a phone call from the police.

It was late when the call came, right after Mark had gone to bed and the children had settled into their rooms. Sarah, who had been reading in the living room, answered the phone, her voice still groggy from a nap.

"Mrs. Martin?" the voice on the other end was stern, yet oddly polite. "We're calling from the police department. We have a few questions regarding a vehicle rental involving your family."

At first, Sarah was confused. What could the police possibly want with her? Her mind raced, trying to connect the dots. But when the officer explained, her stomach dropped, her hands shaking as the words filtered into her consciousness.

"We believe your vehicle, a grey sedan, was used in a series of kidnappings that occurred last month. The car was found near one of the sites where a woman was abducted. Do you have any idea where the car was recently? Was anyone using it?"

The question hit like a physical blow. Sarah's heart seemed to stop in her chest. "Wait... *what*? That's impossible! Daniel—he's just a renter. He's been using the car for work!"

The officer was patient, but his tone darkened. "We're investigating further, ma'am. There have been several cases linked to the car. Please do not leave your home. We'll be sending someone over to speak with you."

The phone clicked, and Sarah was left staring at the screen, her mind a swirl of confusion and dread. The air in the room grew thick, suffocating, as if the house was closing in on her. She tried calling Daniel's number, but the calls went unanswered. Panic began to rise in her chest, the feeling of being utterly helpless sinking deeper with each passing second.

When the police arrived an hour later, they didn't need to explain much further. They had already traced the car's GPS history, which led them to places she never would have imagined. It was clear that Daniel had been using the car to transport victims—victims who had been abducted and taken to remote locations. The police had already found evidence—small items left behind by the victims—and the fear in their eyes only confirmed the horrors unfolding.

As the officers spoke, Sarah's world felt like it was shattering. She felt like she was drowning in a sea of terror, the weight of it pressing down on her chest. Every detail they uncovered twisted her insides, each revelation more sickening than the last. Daniel had planned this meticulously, and now, his actions had stained her family's life in ways she couldn't undo.

The worst part was the realization that they had been complicit, even if unknowingly. Her family's car had been used to commit horrific acts, and they had been the ones to facilitate it. They had trusted Daniel, allowed him access to their lives, and now, their innocence was gone. The once comforting idea of shared economy had turned into a nightmare, a nightmare that they couldn't escape.

The next few days felt like a fog of disbelief. The media was at their door, trying to catch a glimpse of the family involved in the horror. The house, once their sanctuary, felt like a prison, its walls closing in on them as Sarah and Mark tried to piece together the horrifying truth.

Daniel was arrested, but the damage was done. Their car was confiscated as evidence, and their personal lives became an open book for the world to judge. They found themselves constantly looking over their shoulders, even when they went to the grocery store, wondering if anyone had recognized them, if anyone had heard their story and labeled them as accomplices.

In the following weeks, Sarah's sleep became fractured, filled with nightmares of being trapped in a dark car with the sound of screams in the distance. She would wake in the middle of the night, her heart racing, her breath shallow, as if she were still in that moment—still caught in the horror of their decision.

Mark couldn't take the pressure. The constant media scrutiny, the whispers from neighbors, the guilt that ate away at him... it broke him. Their marriage, once strong, began to fray at the edges as the weight of their involvement in the crime spiraled out of control. The isolation they felt grew until they were no longer a family—they were a unit broken by an event they could never fully escape.

The police investigation turned into a legal nightmare. Every day, there was something new—an email, a letter, a phone call—reminding them of the terror Daniel had caused and how their innocent trust had allowed it to unfold. Their house, once full of life and laughter, became a hollow shell of what it had been. They moved out, but there was no escape from the feeling that something terrible had followed them.

It wasn't just the guilt. It was the realization that they had unknowingly been dragged into something far darker than they could have ever imagined. The consequences of their decision to share their car—an innocent choice in the eyes of the world—had shattered their lives.

And as the months passed, Sarah and Mark realized there was no escape from the lingering nightmare. Their lives would always carry the stain of what happened. They would never feel safe again. The consequences of the shared economy were not just financial—they were irreversible.

"The Guest"

The Weston family had always been close. Their small home, nestled in a quiet neighborhood, had always been a place of warmth and comfort. Mark and Olivia, along with their two young children, Lily and Jonah, had lived in the house for years, filling it with laughter and memories. Life had been simple, peaceful. But when Mark lost his job, the burden of bills weighed heavily on them. That's when Olivia suggested they rent out the spare bedroom. It seemed harmless enough—extra income, a little help during a tough time.

The ad went up online, and before long, a man named Samuel reached out. He was in his late forties, polite, well-spoken, and appeared to be in need of a temporary place to stay. He worked as a freelance researcher, he said, and his job required him to travel often. He promised he'd be out of the house most days, only needing the room to sleep. He seemed harmless enough—quiet, introverted, the kind of tenant they could easily share their space with.

At first, everything went well. Samuel was punctual with his rent payments, kept to himself, and rarely intruded on their family time. He spent most of his hours in his room, his door always closed, which didn't seem strange at first. The kids barely noticed him, only seeing him in passing when they'd walk past his door to get to the bathroom or kitchen.

But as the weeks went on, Olivia began to notice small things. The house felt off—noises in the middle of the night, creaks in the floorboards, whispers that seemed to come from nowhere. When she would check on the kids, sometimes she would find them sitting in the dark, staring at the walls, eyes wide with a strange, vacant look, as if they were waiting for something.

One evening, after the kids had gone to bed, Olivia was cleaning up in the kitchen when she heard a sound coming from Samuel's room. It was faint at first—just a small scuffling noise, as if something was being dragged across the floor. It wasn't unusual for him to be moving furniture or organizing his things, but this sound felt *wrong*. It was like a scraping, a slow, deliberate motion.

Curious and unsettled, she went to his door. Hesitating for only a moment, she knocked gently. There was no answer. Just the same unnerving scraping sound. Olivia turned the handle, slowly pushing the door open.

Inside, the room was dim, lit only by the low glow of a desk lamp. Samuel was hunched over his desk, his back to her. He didn't seem to hear her. Olivia stood frozen in the doorway as she saw what he was doing.

He was writing in a thick, leather-bound journal. The pages were filled with strange symbols—mysterious, intricate designs that made no sense. His handwriting was frenzied, wild, and as he wrote, he muttered to himself in a low, almost inaudible voice. But what really caught Olivia's eye were the photographs pinned to the wall—photos of her children, Lily and Jonah, in various states of distress. Some showed them asleep, others captured them in moments of confusion or fear.

Olivia's heart stopped. *How had he gotten these photos? Why were they on his wall?*

Her breath caught in her throat as she backed away from the door, but just before she turned to leave, Samuel spoke, his voice icy and calm.

"You should have known," he said, never looking up from his journal. "This was always going to happen. You never should have let me in."

Olivia's legs felt weak, and her pulse thundered in her ears. She barely registered her own panic as she stumbled back into the hallway, her mind racing. She had to find Mark. She had to get the kids out of the house.

But when she went to the children's rooms, she found something even worse.

Lily was lying motionless in her bed, her eyes wide open but unblinking. Jonah was sitting in his room, rocking back and forth, his hands trembling. Neither of them seemed to acknowledge her presence. It was as if they were in a trance.

A sick feeling crawled up Olivia's spine as she rushed to them, shaking Lily awake. The girl blinked, disoriented, as if she hadn't seen her mother in days. "Mom... they're here," Lily whispered, her voice barely a murmur. "They're watching."

Olivia's heart plummeted. *They?* Who was watching?

A knock on the door shattered the silence. Olivia turned sharply, but before she could react, Samuel appeared in the hallway, blocking her way. His eyes gleamed with something dark and cold. He wasn't the man she had allowed into her home. He wasn't just a guest. He had been planning this, manipulating them all along.

"You've seen too much now," he said, his voice laced with quiet malice. "But it's not over yet. They need to finish."

Before Olivia could scream or run, Samuel's hand shot out, grabbing her by the wrist, pulling her back toward the stairway. She struggled, but his grip was unyielding. "Stay with me, Olivia. You've been so helpful, haven't you? Your children are just the beginning. They're the perfect candidates."

The room began to spin as the realization struck her like a physical blow. Samuel wasn't just staying in their house—he had been performing *experiments* on their children. He had been using them as subjects, watching them, documenting their every movement, studying them in some grotesque, twisted way. The symbols, the photos, the strange mutterings—they were all part of some sickening plan.

A horrifying thought gnawed at Olivia's mind: *How long had this been going on? What had he done to them?*

Just then, the air in the house seemed to shift. Olivia's vision blurred as she heard the sound of footsteps. Heavy, deliberate steps, getting closer. More people, coming from the shadows, filing out of the corners of the house, their faces hidden behind masks. She saw the faint glint of knives in the dim light.

Her body shook with terror as she realized there was no escape. The house had become a laboratory, a place of twisted experimentation, and she and her family were its unwilling subjects. The door to freedom was locked behind them, and Samuel's guests were the ones who held the keys.

In a flash, Olivia was struck with the crushing weight of despair. She had let this man into her home, trusted him with their lives, and now they were trapped in a nightmare from which there was no waking.

As the strangers closed in, and Samuel's cold gaze followed her every movement, Olivia's last thought was that this was the end. She had tried to protect her children, but she had failed. There was no escape from the horrors they had unknowingly invited in.

The world outside the walls no longer mattered. They were part of it now—part of the experiment, part of the twisted game, and they would never leave.

"The Surgeon in the Yard"

Anna and Tom had always been the type of people who liked to help others. They had a spacious house with a large backyard, perfect for hosting barbecues or relaxing on weekends. The extra space was a luxury, and when money became tight after Tom's job cutback, they decided to rent out the backyard to help cover the mortgage.

It wasn't the first time they had considered using the space for extra income. With the rise of shared economy platforms, renting out space seemed to be the easiest and most practical option. They listed the area online for gardening, small events, or even for people who just wanted to escape the bustle of city life for a little while. They didn't expect anything unusual to happen.

That was before Daniel showed up.

He was a man in his late forties, well-dressed but slightly disheveled, with a face that seemed perpetually tired. He claimed he was a medical professional looking for a quiet place to operate a small private practice. He assured Anna and Tom that his work was legitimate. He had "patients" who needed help in a calm, private environment, and the backyard seemed like the perfect, secluded spot. He offered to pay in advance, and with the stress of their financial situation, Anna and Tom reluctantly agreed.

At first, everything seemed harmless. Daniel set up a small tent in the far corner of the yard, next to the trees. He placed some medical equipment there—a few chairs, a table, sterile drapes. Tom assumed Daniel was a legitimate practitioner, albeit a bit eccentric. It seemed like a harmless arrangement, just a man doing his job in the privacy of the backyard.

But then things began to feel... wrong.

It started with the sounds. Anna was the first to notice them late at night—soft, muffled screams that seemed to emanate from the direction of the backyard. She had convinced herself it was the wind at first, rustling through the trees, or perhaps someone talking loudly in the distance. But as the days passed, the screams grew more distinct, more unsettling. There was something desperate in the way the sounds cut through the silence of the night, like someone in pain—or someone trying to suppress their agony.

She tried to ignore it. After all, it wasn't her business, was it? Daniel had told them it was a medical practice, even if it seemed to operate at odd hours. But the fear kept growing, creeping into her every thought. The quiet hum of the generator in the backyard started to disturb her sleep. It was always there, buzzing relentlessly, never turning off.

One evening, as Anna walked out into the yard to check on the garden, she noticed something strange. The tent was open, a dim light spilling out into the yard. She was used to the shadows of the night, but this light was different—sharp, unnatural, like a surgical lamp casting eerie shadows on the grass. For the briefest moment, Anna thought she saw someone moving inside the tent—a figure lying on the table, their body limp, as if they were unconscious or restrained.

Her heart skipped a beat as she quickly turned away, her footsteps quickening. She didn't know what to make of it, but she knew she had to talk to Tom.

That night, she woke up to find him already pacing the living room. His face was pale, his eyes wide with disbelief. He had found something that had completely shattered his understanding of the situation.

Tom had been out in the yard earlier in the day, trying to fix a broken sprinkler. When he'd walked near the tent, he had noticed blood stains on the ground, leading away from the entrance. At first, he thought it was just something from a wild animal. But the sight of a syringe discarded near the tent, and the unmistakable smell of antiseptic, had made his stomach churn. His heart raced as he realized what had been happening right under their noses.

"Anna, we need to call the police," Tom said, his voice low, trembling. "He's been performing surgeries—*illegal* surgeries. I found medical records, even patient notes. He's... he's doing something terrible back there."

Anna's chest tightened. The realization hit her with full force. The screams in the night. The strange, distant figures. The blood. It wasn't just some harmless medical practice. It was a nightmare, a twisted operation taking place in their own yard.

The next morning, when Anna and Tom confronted Daniel, he denied everything at first. But the truth came out slowly, like a slow burn, as they pushed harder. Daniel revealed that he wasn't just performing minor procedures. He had been conducting unlicensed, illegal surgeries—botched procedures that had left his patients scarred or worse. He had been performing experiments in the name of "medical advancement," using unapproved drugs, dangerous methods, and, disturbingly, involving people who were desperate enough to put themselves in his hands.

The more Daniel spoke, the more their house felt like a prison. His calm demeanor was terrifying, as though he had no remorse for what he had done. He wasn't apologetic—he was smug. He had been operating out of sight, knowing that no one would stop him, hiding behind the walls of their own trust.

"You don't understand," Daniel said with a faint smile. "You gave me a place to do what was needed. You opened the door. I've been providing a service to people who need it. You should be grateful."

His words rattled in Anna's skull as she felt her stomach turn. The house, once full of warmth, had become a chamber of horrors. The walls felt too close, the windows too small, the air too thick with the weight of the terror that had been unfolding in the shadows.

But even worse was the realization that they were now part of the operation. They had allowed it to happen. The very space they had trusted had been turned into a medical dungeon. Their backyard—once a place of simple summer evenings—had become the setting for human suffering. The realization that their lives had been shattered by their own naivety left them broken.

Tom immediately contacted the authorities, but by the time the police arrived, Daniel had vanished. The tent was gone, the blood washed away, and there was no trace of him or his twisted experiments. But the damage had already been done. The police found medical files, photographs of surgeries, and notes on unapproved procedures, all hidden in the small, makeshift office in the tent. It was clear that Daniel had been operating for months, possibly years, and no one had even suspected.

The fallout from Daniel's operations spread far and wide. Victims came forward, their bodies marred by surgeries gone wrong, their lives irrevocably changed. Anna and Tom's lives crumbled under the weight of the scandal. The once tight-knit community turned against them, blaming them for allowing it all to happen. The neighbors whispered, the press hounded them, and the authorities deemed them guilty by association.

The house, once full of life and love, became a tomb—a constant reminder of the horrors that had been allowed to fester in the dark corners of their lives. The memories of the man in their backyard, the surgeries, the blood, and the agonized cries haunted them forever. They had trusted a stranger, shared their space, and now there was no escaping the consequences.

The walls of their home, once filled with hope, now felt suffocating, pressing in on them, a constant reminder of the nightmare that had taken root in the very soil of their lives.

And as they packed their things, preparing to leave the house that had once been their sanctuary, they knew one thing for certain: the horrors of the shared economy would follow them forever.

"The Stranger in the House"

Daniel had always been a cautious man, a man who believed in the sanctity of trust and the goodness of people. When he first posted the ad for his spare bedroom online, he never imagined it would lead him down such a dark path. The house had once been a place of warmth—shared with his wife and children, filled with laughter and the scent of home-cooked meals. But after the divorce, the house had grown quieter, emptier, a silent reminder of everything he had lost. Renting out the extra room seemed like a simple solution, a way to make some extra money and keep the house in good shape.

When Laura responded to his ad, she seemed like the perfect fit. In her early thirties, with soft features and a gentle demeanor, she came across as approachable and kind. She was moving to the city for a new job, she said, and just needed a temporary place to stay while she got settled. There was something disarming about her, something in her soft smile that made Daniel feel instantly at ease. She offered to pay a few months' rent upfront, and in the end, the deal was done.

At first, everything seemed perfect. Laura was quiet and respectful, keeping to herself most of the time. She didn't make a lot of noise or interfere with Daniel's routine. She would leave for work in the morning, only to return late at night, sometimes with a take-out dinner in hand. She would smile politely, nodding at Daniel as they passed in the hallway, but their interactions remained surface-level. For a while, it was just like any other arrangement—a stranger sharing space with a family, an unremarkable coexistence.

But things started to shift, slowly at first, in ways that Daniel couldn't quite explain.

It began with small things. Daniel's wallet, which he usually left on the kitchen counter, was found in a different place. His car keys would be moved when he was sure he hadn't touched them. His credit card bill came with strange charges—an expensive restaurant meal, hotel bookings, and other items he didn't recognize. At first, he thought he was just being careless, distracted by work and the stress of his personal life. But as the days passed, the unease began to grow.

Then came the phone calls.

He would hear Laura talking late into the night, her voice low and urgent, but when he tried to listen more closely, she always cut the conversation short. He overheard bits and pieces—something about "getting him to trust me," "it's all going according to plan," and "soon, everything will be ours." Every time he walked past her room, there was the faint scent of perfume, but something about it was too sweet, too cloying, like a trap that was just waiting to snap shut.

Daniel tried to confront Laura once, asking her directly if there was something wrong. She gave him a soft, reassuring smile, brushing off his concerns with an explanation that sounded too practiced, too perfect. "Oh, don't worry, Daniel. It's just work stress. You know how it is—sometimes you have to take risks to make things happen."

She didn't tell him much about her job, which seemed odd. She was always vague about the details, but she was so pleasant, so believable. Daniel, despite his gut feeling that something wasn't right, kept giving her the benefit of the doubt. She was just a renter, after all.

But as the weeks wore on, Daniel began to notice things he couldn't ignore. His bank accounts were drained—small, incremental withdrawals that didn't seem to make sense. He had accounts set up to track every expense, but it was as if the numbers never added up, as if something invisible was siphoning away his resources. His mail began disappearing, important letters he never received, only to find them months later in Laura's room, carefully tucked away in a drawer.

Then came the final straw.

One evening, when Daniel was cleaning out the attic, he found a stack of paperwork he didn't recognize. Among the papers, there were legal documents—contracts and fake identification cards, documents that clearly belonged to other people, not Laura. He stared at the papers for a long time, his mind whirling with the implications. These were *fraudulent documents*, and they had been carefully hidden in his home. Laura wasn't just a harmless tenant. She was running a scam, and he had been an unwitting accomplice.

Fear gripped Daniel's chest as he realized the truth. Laura had been playing him from the very beginning, weaving her web of deceit with calm precision. He had been her mark, her ticket to the life she wanted to live. She had lied, manipulated, and stolen from him in ways he couldn't even fully comprehend.

The worst part was that Laura wasn't just taking money from him. She had been using the trust he had given her to destroy his life. She had manipulated his children, too. They had started acting differently—more secretive, less trusting. There were moments when they would look at him with strange expressions, as if they knew something he didn't, as if they had already been pulled into her dark scheme.

The turning point came when Daniel tried to confront her once more. This time, it was not with questions, but with accusations. As he entered her room, his voice shaking with anger, he demanded answers. He found her sitting calmly at her desk, a laptop open in front of her. The screen flickered as she smiled up at him, her eyes cold, calculating.

"It's too late for you, Daniel," she said, her voice dripping with honeyed venom. "I've already secured everything I need. Your money, your trust, your family—they're all part of my plan."

Daniel's heart pounded in his chest. He couldn't move. His feet felt like they were cemented to the floor as he stared at the woman who had destroyed him.

"You were never just a landlord to me," Laura continued, her voice soft and persuasive. "You were the bridge to everything I wanted. And now, I have it all. Your house. Your resources. Your future."

The realization slammed into Daniel like a freight train. Laura had been using him to fund her operations, to secure her life, and to manipulate everyone around him. And now, it was all falling apart. His home, his family, his life—they were all ruined.

And there was nothing he could do.

As Laura turned back to her laptop, casually typing away, Daniel understood the full extent of his fate. The web of deceit was far too intricate, far too widespread for him to fight. The damage was done. His home was no longer his own. Laura had taken everything—his trust, his money, his family—and left him with nothing but the wreckage of a life that was no longer his.

There was no escape.

Get Another Book Free

[1]

We love writing and have produced many books.

As a thank you for being one of our amazing readers, we'd like to offer you a free book.

To claim this limited-time offer, visit the site below and enter your name and email address.

You'll receive one of our great books directly to your email, completely free!

https://free.copypeople.com

---

1. https://free.copypeople.com

Did you love *Horrors We Shared The Risks of the Shared Economy*?
Then you should read *Digital Hell: When Brain and Machine Become One*[2] by CopyPeople!

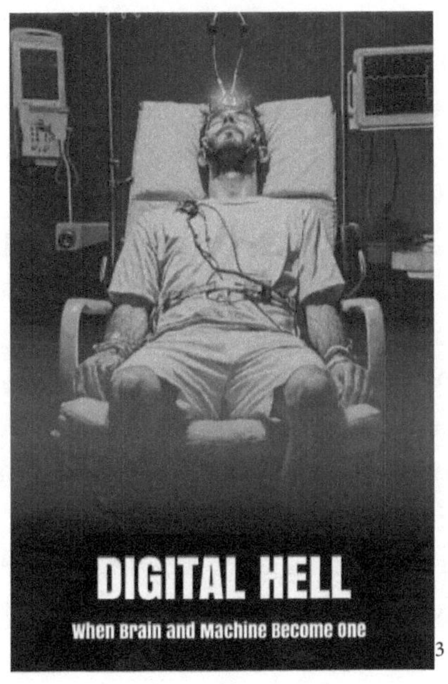

In a future where the line between humanity and technology has blurred, **Digital Hell: When Brain and Machine Become One** takes you on a chilling journey into the dark, horrifying consequences of connecting the human mind to machines. This collection of unsettling short stories explores the terrifying, irreversible impacts of brain-computer interfaces as they go horribly wrong, leaving their victims trapped in an endless nightmare of their own creation.

---

2. https://books2read.com/u/bWLOZ1

3. https://books2read.com/u/bWLOZ1

Imagine a world where your thoughts can be hacked, your memories stolen, and your deepest fears broadcast to the world. In this anthology, you'll meet characters who dared to embrace the promise of advanced neural technology—only to find themselves caught in a web of digital terror they can't escape. From a woman whose thoughts are stolen and sold to the highest bidder, to a man trapped in a virtual hell with no way out, each story delves into the madness that unfolds when mind and machine are no longer separate entities.

With every turn of the page, **Digital Hell** challenges the notion of what it means to be human. Each tale explores the dark side of human nature, as well as the existential consequences of tampering with the brain's intricate systems. What happens when your thoughts are no longer your own? What if the technology meant to enhance your life instead destroys it, trapping you in an unending nightmare?

From malfunctioning brain chips that turn the world into a sensory overload to digital prisons where consciousness is forever confined, these stories explore a range of mind-bending scenarios that will leave you questioning the price of technological progress. Will you be able to escape the digital abyss, or will you become one with the machine?

Every story in **Digital Hell** is a unique, horrifying exploration of the darker side of artificial intelligence, cybernetics, and virtual realities. Whether it's the terrifying reality of thought exposure, the haunting consequences of memory manipulation, or the existential horror of losing one's identity in the digital ether, this book will captivate fans of psychological horror, sci-fi thrillers, and dystopian fiction alike.

In a world increasingly dependent on technology, **Digital Hell** serves as a stark warning of the dangers we may face as we push the boundaries of human cognition. The stories within these pages are not only about the collapse of individuals but about the moral, social, and psychological costs of merging the mind with machines.

Get ready to plunge into a realm where the virtual and the real collide with terrifying results. **Digital Hell: When Brain and Machine Become One** will leave you haunted, unsettled, and questioning the true cost of technological advancement. Will you dare to face the horrors that await within?

Prepare to enter a world where the greatest threat to your mind is the machine you've trusted to enhance it.

Also by Morgan B. Blake

The Hidden Truth
Silent Obsession

Standalone
Temporal Havoc
The AI Resurrection
99942 Apophis
The Shadows We Keep
Whispers of the Forgotten
Christmas Chronicles: Enchanted Stories for the Holiday Season
Realm of Enchantment Tales from the Mystic Lands
The Taniwha's Secret
Unicorn Magic Discovering the Wonders of a Hidden World
Vampire's Vow: Stories of Blood and Betrayal
Legends of the Damned: Villains Who Defied Fate and Conquered All
Twisted Affection: How Love Can Break You
Lethal Beauty Inside the Minds of Women Who Kill
No One Left Behind Escaping the Shadow of War
The Spirit of Christmas: Heartwarming Stories of Holiday Magic
Forever Friends: Heartbreaking and Touching Dog Stories
Phantom Footsteps Stories from the Dark Corners of the Mind

The Christmas Deception Unmasking the Dark Truth of Santa
The Hidden Code Unlocking Ancient Mysteries
Rotting Streets The Collapse of Civilization
Beneath the Christmas Tree Dark and Enchanting Tales
The Witching Hour Ghostly Tales of Sorcery
Whispers of Magic: Enchanting Tales from Fairy Realms
Shattered Idols: The Dark Truths of Fame
Horrors We Shared The Risks of the Shared Economy